Buck Me

Ashley Willow

A BOULDER RANCH NOVEL

BUCK ME

ASHLEY WILLOW

Book Cover by Isabelle Olmo

Editor: Tara McGee

First edition 2025

Boulder Ranch

Buck Me by Ashley Willow
Love Me by Ashley Willow
Hunt Me by Ashley Willow
Ride Me by Britton Brinkley
Want Me by Britton Brinkley
Save Me by Britton Brinkley

Buck Me Playlist

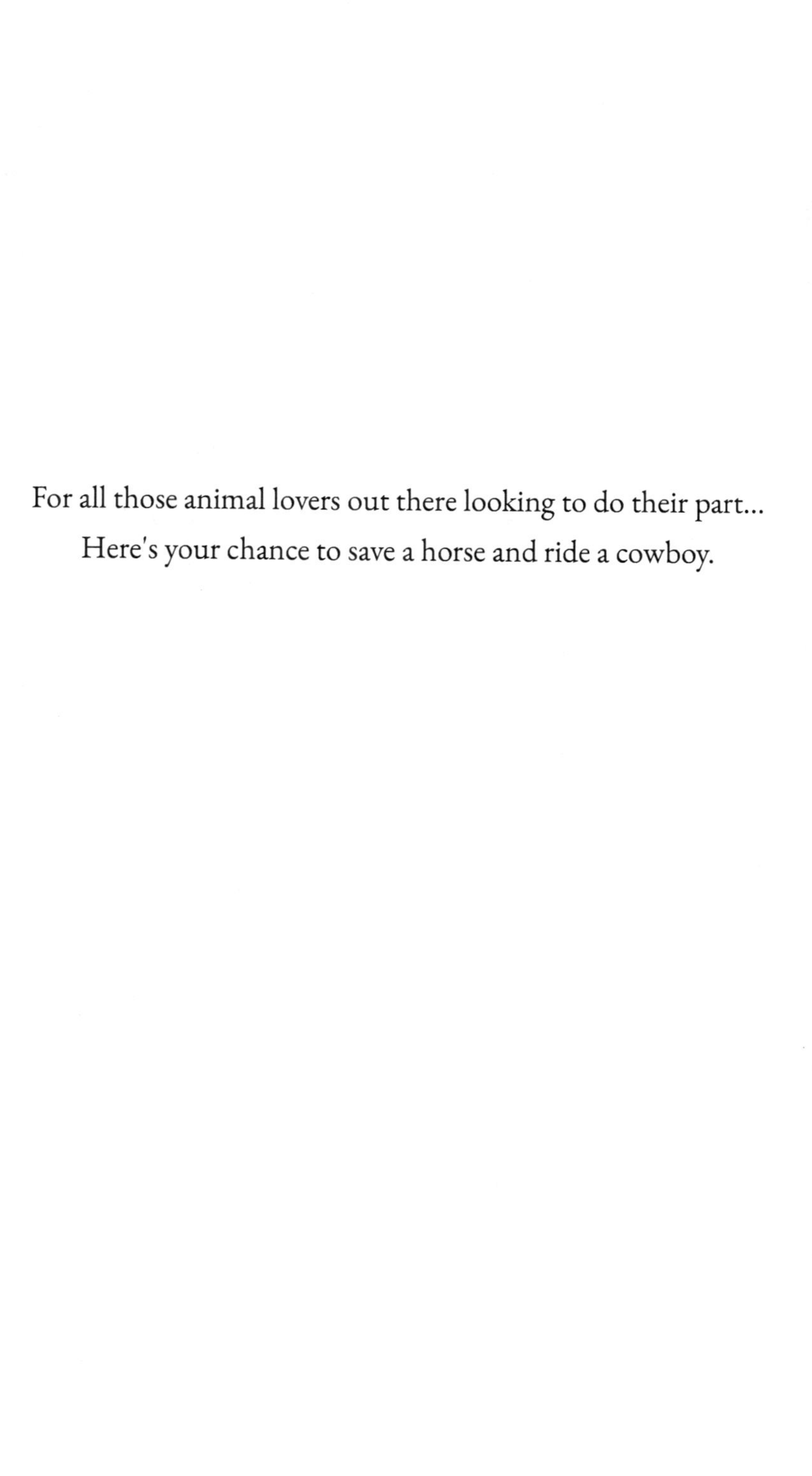

For all those animal lovers out there looking to do their part…

Here's your chance to save a horse and ride a cowboy.

Chapter 1

Joy

I'm running late, of course. Running late is kind of my thing. If it isn't work, or someplace I *have* to be, I'm probably going to get there whenever I get there. Rayna is never going to believe that I really did leave the house right after she asked me to meet her for lunch. As soon as we got off the phone, she sent me a text message telling me to hurry up because she's starving. Leave it to her to get me out of the house on my day off and then rush me on top of that. I headed straight to the market for two of our favorite smoked turkey melts. But then I ran into Mrs. Crawley, and she wouldn't stop talking about some "young man who loves exotic women" and that she wants to introduce us.

Exotic? I laugh again as I round the turn into the parking lot of the doctor's office. My skin may be brown, and I may have curly hair, but I'm hardly exotic. I'm as American as Mrs. Crawley. No fun accent. No fun recipes. Just regular, boring me. But then again, I suppose coming from outside of Cole County might make me a bit of a novelty for this small town.

As soon as I pull into the parking lot, a pickup starts backing up, heading right for me. I lay on the horn, trying to make myself known, but it does nothing. Short of backing into the street, there's nowhere for me to go. As predicted, the truck hits the front of my car hard enough to move me.

"What the hell!" I shout as I slam my door shut and walk around to see if my fender is lying on the ground.

By the time I make it over to inspect the damage, the driver's side door opens, and I watch as a cowboy boot connects with the ground. The driver steps the rest of the way out, and my breath catches. I'm looking up at what is definitely the most good-looking man I've seen out in the wild. Tall. Thick, dark curls show from beneath his cowboy hat. He has a neatly trimmed beard, with traces of silver.

"I'm sorry. Are you okay?" He takes his hat off and raises his hands in apology.

I continue to study his face. Perfectly sculpted lips, a strong nose, and the most gorgeous honey-brown eyes. Reminding myself that he asked a question, I give my head a gentle shake.

"I'm fine. No thanks to you," I grumble.

He returns his brown Stetson to his head then absently rubs the bandage covering his hand as he looks from my car and back to me. "Listen. I said I'm sorry; do you need my blood too? I'm not trying to be a dick, but I'm having a shit day, and I just want to get home. Your car seems okay."

I glance over at my car and the glaring lack of damage. I'm not sure how, but the only thing I can see wrong is the tiniest scratch. Almost beginning to pity him, I feel my face begin to soften for a moment... until I remember how he just kept backing up as I blared the horn.

"It looks like my car is fine. But pay attention to what you're doing before you kill somebody."

He mumbles something under his breath as I turn to head back to the driver's seat. After making sure there's no one coming up behind me, I back up, giving him plenty of space to pull out of the spot and out of the parking lot. As I watch his truck turn onto the road, the familiar feeling of regret begins to sneak back in. My car is fine. I'm fine. It wasn't necessary to act like such a bitch to the guy. But he really does need to pay attention.

"I knew you weren't anywhere near ready to walk out your door," Rayna says from behind the desk before I'm even fully inside.

"I left on time, but I ran into Mrs. Crawley, and you know how she likes to talk. I've been in the parking lot for like ten minutes, though. You didn't hear all that commotion?"

She just blinks at me. "We had a lot of patients in exam rooms at once. I was pretty focused on getting the rooms cleaned up and the right notes in for the right patients. There could have been an explosion, and I wouldn't have heard anything."

"Well as soon as I pulled into the parking lot, some asshole in a giant truck backed into me."

Rayna takes the bags of food from me, and we head to the break room. I accept my daily dose of jealousy at the way she looks in her scrubs. She's one of those people who fills out every outfit to perfection. On top of that, she can throw on a pair of earrings and some lip gloss and look photo ready no matter what she has on. Meanwhile, I look like a potato in my scrubs—plain and shapeless.

I work part time at the Family Health Center as a medical assistant, and here I am on my day off, bringing lunch and hanging out. Rayna's my best friend, and I would have been bored just sitting at home, anyway. We're entering rodeo season, so there won't be much time to meet up for lunch or to do much of anything during the day. Part time at Bolder Ranch becomes full time and then some during the spring and summer, with several of the rodeo participants boarding their horses at the ranch during the season.

"Is your car okay? You seem okay, but are you?" Rayna asks as she takes a seat at the table and divvies up the food. "I'm just glad neither of you stumbled in wounded. I'm already behind."

"I'm fine," I huff, sitting in the seat across from her. "I'm just annoyed. I laid on the horn and everything. Then he acted like I was inconveniencing him. He's the one who backed into me, not the other way around!"

"And you're looking at me like this is my fault."

I laugh, taking a bite of my sandwich, which is delicious, before I answer her. "Well, it certainly isn't mine."

Rayna rolls her eyes and waves me off. "Anyway, are you sure it'll be okay if I'm behind the scenes with you tonight? I don't want you to get in trouble."

It's opening night of the rodeo at Bolder Ranch, and the rodeo kicks off bull riding season. I have to work, but I should be able to watch most of it. Between immediately bonding with Gary and Rhonda Miller, and Gary finding out that Rayna is Wyatt's fiancé, I'm not worried about getting into any trouble.

"Yeah. They suggested it, actually. Gary said it's pretty common, and as long as you're comfortable around horses it's fine."

Rayna stops chewing and quickly swallows. "I don't know anything about horses!"

"I know, but you'll be fine. You'll be with me. Most of my work happens before the event, and I just have to hang around in case they need me."

"I don't see why they would need you during the event at all."

"You never know. A horse could need to be tacked up or untacked in a hurry. Or something else that needs extra hands. It'll be fine," I say in my most convincing voice.

Being relatively new to the town and even newer to the rodeo and bull riding scene, I really don't want to be there alone for my first event. I know this isn't Rayna's thing, so I'm crossing everything that she isn't about to back out.

"Let me borrow a pair of cowboy boots so I can at least look like I belong there."

My mood is a million times lighter knowing she didn't bring me here to cancel. I barely even remember the asshole from the parking lot as I look forward to later. Taking a relieved breath, I lean back in my seat with my arms folded and a grin across my face.

"I'll even let you borrow the beat-up ones to make it more convincing."

Chapter 2

Tate

My truck door slams when I close it with way more force than is necessary. I'm not sure why I keep allowing Grayson to get to me with the same shit over and over. And to the point I backed into a woman's car. Still fuming after slamming the door of my truck, I do the same with my front door to see if that might help. It doesn't.

I barely have time to shower and get changed before heading back to Boulder Ranch. It's opening night, so we don't have to ride, but we're pickup men for the amateur roughstock events. And, somehow, that's my fault too. Grayson's attitude problem is getting really fucking old. I shake my hand to relieve the ache. Thankfully it isn't broken. I knew better than to hit him. Even though I'm not riding tonight, I need to be able to hold the reins, and maybe even toss a rope.

"I don't know why you're always trying to be Dad. He didn't like you either."

Grayson's words echo in my mind. They hurt, but I probably deserved them after possibly breaking his jaw. I squeeze my eyes closed to combat the sting. Fuck. He's been my responsibility for the past fifteen years and, whether he resents it or not, I'm the only family he's got. And he's all I have.

My mind drifts back to the woman in the parking lot as I step into the shower and rush to get clean. She was pissed. But fucking gorgeous even though she definitely wanted to kill me. I shouldn't have hit her car, but she didn't have to get so worked up when there was barely even a scratch. The way she stormed out of her car, curls wild and eyes blazing, you would have thought I aimed for her.

A few minutes later, I'm walking back out the door, my hair still damp and bag in hand. Opening night has always been my favorite, and it's taking everything in me not to let Grayson ruin it. Clenching and unclenching my fist, I fight against the bandage. I'm still pissed that he pushed me that far. Dr. Robinson suggested I take tonight off, but that would be ridiculous. I've made the eight on the back of a bull in worse shape than this.

As I pull into the gravel parking area and reach for my bag, I wish I'd listened to that doctor. Lining up and getting introduced is one thing. Having to be pickup with Grayson when all I want to do is punch him again seems like a recipe for failure.

The weight of my bag on my shoulder and the chaps across my arm remind me that this is it. All I need to do is avoid that asshole as much as possible and I'll be able to enjoy the rest of the night. The event is a big one, and we only have to work together for part of it. I round the corner feeling slightly better about everything. But of course, the first person I lay eyes on is Grayson. Fucking perfect.

CHAPTER 3

JOY

As soon as I step out of the barn, I see Rayna walking across the grass heading away from the parking area and breathe a sigh of relief. Being a ranch hand, no day is exactly the same. I've finished up in the stalls and with the odd jobs and need something to distract me from feeling out of place. I haven't lived here long, moving only after Rayna convinced me to follow her to Cole County. She came here on vacation, met Wyatt, and never returned home.

"Is your man aware of how hot you look? Damn, girl," I tease as soon as she's within earshot. Her flannel shirt is tied at the front, and her bootcut jeans look like they were tailored to fit her. My boots complete the outfit. "I see you found my boots."

"Are these the right ones?" She looks momentarily panicked.

"Yes, you're fine. I wouldn't care what pair you picked. But those are the ones I was talking about. I wore those back when

I used to help out at my aunt's stables. They should be nice and broken in."

My work is complete for now, so I lead Rayna to the gate alongside where the competitors enter for the timed events and climb up to sit on the gate. She hesitates for a moment before climbing up next to me. I can't explain why, but it's this simple act that makes me feel at home on the ranch. My aunt runs stables where they board and train horses. Even though I grew up closer to the city, I spent so many summers with her, helping out where I could, that somehow, this ranch makes me a little less homesick.

Before we can continue the conversation, the screens on either side of the arena light up as the announcer gains the crowd's attention. Goosebumps spread across my flesh as anticipation courses through me. This is my first time at opening night here, but even I can feel the excitement racing through the crowd. Glancing over at Rayna, I can tell she's feeling it too as a grin spreads across her face.

Trinity is carrying the American flag as she rides up next to us to wait. I've been to enough events in general to have an idea of what to expect. Lights flash as a slideshow begins. I grip Rayna's hand in pure excitement as grainy images of cowboys and barrel racers flicker across the screens. As the music plays, my eyes remain glued to the images. Highlights of years past. My breath hitches when they stop on a photo of a saddle bronc rider, one arm raised to the sky as he holds on to the rigging. Even with his hat hiding most of his face, I can practically see his scowl of concentration. I know that face.

When they announce the last year of Boulder Ranch under ownership of the Miller family, the crowd gasps. I've barely registered what's been said when Trinity leads her horse around the track, flag held high, as a voice begins singing the National Anthem. The crowd stands in silence, keeping their eyes on the flag as the woman finishes singing.

"Not going to lie; I'm beyond excited," Rayna squeals, gripping my hand.

The announcer begins speaking, but I'm not really paying attention. The fact that I'm here and a part of the event that brings the town together is more than I'm ready to think about. I'm from the suburbs. Even though a lot of things seem to be the same no matter where we come from, there's nothing quite like the excitement of a small town.

The announcer begins introducing each contestant, including those competing in the next day's events. From what I gathered, opening night features all but the pro roughstock competitors. A group of men and women line up, stepping forward as their names are called.

"Tate Garrison," the announcer continues, as the next person in line steps forward, removing his hat and waving it toward the crowd.

"Wait a minute," I hiss, quickly gaining Rayna's attention. "That's him. That's the asshole who backed into me."

"Tate Garrison?"

I snap my gaze to my friend. "Yeah?"

"Tate. Garrison." She enunciates each syllable, causing my skin to crawl. "Oh, my god."

At this point, I'm annoyed that I seem to be missing something. Why does she keep repeating herself? Yes. Tate fucking Garrison. It's obvious by the way she stares at me that the name is important. In no mood for any back and forth, I wait for her to get to the point.

Before she begins her explanation, my gaze drifts back to the lineup and straight into Tate's whiskey-brown eyes. I could get lost in them even at this distance. He gives me a nod before turning to exit the arena with the rest of the group. And I'm left trying to figure out why I'm suddenly breathless.

"Tate Garrison is the best bronc rider this arena has seen. And he only competes here because he retired from bull riding. He's a PBR World Champion."

My eyes snap to the arena and then back to Rayna. "How do you know this? You've never even been here before. And you just moved here!"

She laughs and shrugs her shoulders. "I work at the only local doctor's office. I know everything. But seriously, everyone knows that. He's basically a local legend."

Of course he is. And I was a total bitch to him. I groan inwardly, trying to figure out how I haven't seen him around the ranch. Most of the riders who compete throughout the season stop by to at least ride during the week, and I would have remembered him. Before I can say anything in response, the pickup men make their entrance through the gate, riding in at an easy trot. It's Tate and another equally attractive man.

"Damn."

"Right?" Rayna agrees, letting me know I said that out loud. "Those two are brothers. That other guy is Grayson. He's a bull rider. And they don't get along."

I laugh. Of course, Rayna knows all about what's going on at a place she's never even been. I watch as Tate sits relaxed on the horse, holding the reins with one hand, and resting his free arm across his lap. There is something about a man on a horse...

"I'll never understand why people seek medical advice only to ignore all said advice."

I look down to find the rodeo doctor standing with her hands on her hips, glaring daggers at the Garrison brothers. It's obvious one, or both, shouldn't be out there. I look back toward the guys in time to see Tate flexing and unflexing his right hand. The hand that was covered in a bandage when he left the doctor's office.

"I take it Grayson was also advised to take the night off?" Rayna asks with a laugh.

"You know I can't talk about it. But how stubborn can two people be?" Dr. Thompson replies before heading off to the other side of the arena.

I assume whatever they are talking about must have to do with Tate being at the doctor's office earlier. If it's drama, I'll hear about it. I might keep to myself because I don't know anyone very well, but no one else around the place seems to keep anything to themselves. Ever.

The events get started but I'm having a hard time watching anything other than Tate's body as it sways on the back of the horse. Or the way he twirls the rope while wrangling the livestock that aren't interested in going back into the pen. If it wasn't for the occasional question from Rayna, I wouldn't be paying any attention to the actual events at all.

"So? Are you going to treat me to the whole experience, or what?" Rayna asks, snapping me out of my haze as the night draws to a close.

I blink at her, having no idea what she's talking about. Dr. Thompson, who has joined us where we are now standing along the gate, is also watching me expectantly. "I don't know, what's the whole experience?"

"The Thirsty Pony! Drinks. Line dancing. Cowboys," Rayna explains, as if I should know this already.

"Is that really a thing?" I ask in surprise.

I hear a chuckle and see Dr. Thompson trying her best not to laugh. "I assume you must be going, Dr. Thompson? Since you're over here laughing at me."

"Oh, no. Please call me River. And I didn't really plan on it..."

"You should totally come. Enjoy the 'whole experience' with us," I invite. "We'll meet you there as soon as I finish up here."

"Okay. I guess," she answers as Rayna silently cheers in the background.

Chapter 4

Joy

As soon as we step into the Thirsty Pony, Rayna lets out an excited squeal and drags me to the bar. It's packed, but she manages to squeeze us into an empty space and orders shots. Lemon drops. I haven't had one of those since college, and I turn to argue with her as soon as I recall why. Instant flashbacks of hugging the toilet bowl all night begin playing in fast motion across my mind.

"I don't want to hear it," Rayna says before I even open my mouth. "We're having a good time. I'm off tomorrow, and you only have to help out with morning chores tomorrow before going back for the event. Let's pretend we're twenty-something again. Wyatt already said he'll pick us up if we need him to."

Finding zero holes in her argument, I shrug and accept the shot glass, downing it like a pro. Of course, we follow the shot with a loud cheer like a couple of drunken college girls. I laugh and go with it. Why not? I only get to live once. A few seats down from where we're standing, I spot River nursing a drink. Flagging down the bartender, I order another round and include River.

"Let's dance!" I suggest loudly enough for River to hear.

She doesn't say no, so I grab her by the arm and drag her to the center of the dance floor. Do I know this line dance? Nope, but two shots of vodka have already given me enough courage to follow along and learn as I go. As the warmth from the alcohol begins to settle over me, I give myself permission to live in the moment. If Rayna wants to relive the drunken college years, who am I to step in and ruin it?

They have been playing song after song that I know. The music pulses through me as I forget about everything else. Finally, the tempo slows, and I open my eyes, preparing to leave the dance floor, when a large, callused hand grips my arm. Whipping my head around, I once again collide gazes with Tate Garrison.

"Hey." His rough voice is barely loud enough for me to hear.

"Hi."

"May I have this dance? I owe you at least that for backing into your car earlier."

My brain fails me, leaving me incapable of forming a coherent response. Of course, my traitorous brain would choose this moment to give up. I fumble for a moment before finally nodding in agreement. And then I'm in his arms. He's so tall. And so... big. My head barely reaches his shoulder as he pulls me close and sways to the music. Rascal Flats plays over the speakers as I manage to keep step with him. He smells woodsy and clean. And safe.

"I think I owe you an apology," he says softly into my ear. "I was distracted earlier. I'm sorry we met that way. And I'm sorry if I was an asshole."

"No," I argue. "I'm the one who owes you an apology. I was a bitch. I'm fine. My car is fine. There's no reason I should have spoken to you the way I did."

Tate says nothing. He simply pulls me close and continues moving to the music. At this point, I have no idea what's happening, so I just go with it. Tate hasn't even introduced himself, not that I don't already know exactly who he is. But for some reason, this seems like the perfect apology that I don't deserve. When the song ends, he ducks down to meet my gaze.

"Let's start over. I'm Tate Garrison. It's a pleasure to meet you."

I blink several times before looking down at his outstretched hand and accepting it. "Joy Anderson."

His smile causes my knees to go weak. Crinkles form around his eyes and creases accentuate his dimples, making them noticeable even beneath his beard. And his mouth—god, that mouth. Perfectly sculpted lips have me quickly imagining what they might feel like.

"Let me buy you a drink," I blurt, desperate to fill the silence between us. "I owe you one for how rude I was earlier."

"Nope. We aren't going to bring up what happened earlier again. This is our first meeting." Once more, he flashes those honey-brown eyes at me, and I don't even remember my name. "But a drink sounds perfect."

"A round of lemon drops!" I announce as soon as the bartender is within earshot. "And a round of whatever the men are drinking!"

The bartender takes the credit card that I've produced from—well—I'm not even sure where it came from. All I know is that I'm doing everything I can to continue being wild and free when all I want to do is figure out everything there is to know about the man beside me.

"Jack and Coke for me," Tate says to the bartender as he stuffs a twenty into the tip jar.

"Grayson's been drinking Miller Light if you really want him on your tab," the bartender says as she fills two shot glasses before mixing Tate's Jack and Coke.

I look around the room and don't see Grayson anywhere. Or River. "Well, if they turn up serve them a drink on my tab."

"Are you good?" Rayna asks me. "Wyatt is on his way to pick me up. Do you need a ride?"

"I've got her," Tate answers before I've even had a chance to respond. "This will only be my second drink of the night. And my last. Wyatt knows me. He'll tell you I'm trustworthy."

I don't fight through the haze of alcohol when Tate pulls me into his arms and leads me to the dance floor. I don't even attempt to argue with him. Once again, I'm in his warm embrace. His hands roam my body as we move to the music. My side. My back. My waist. My skin tingles each place he touches, yet somehow, he isn't touching me enough.

The beat picks up, and so do our movements, blending in with the feeling of Tate's hands along my flesh. My mind usually likes to come up with every possible worst-case scenario. But as Tate's body warms mine, I refuse to think of anything besides this moment. The vibration of my body under his delicious touch is enough to make me forget about the world.

"Let me take you home."

The request seems strange in my hazy mind. I know I'm not capable of driving myself home, but there's something telling me I should have left with Rayna. Something I'm not sure I should listen to, but as my eyes focus on his serious gaze and firmly set jaw, I'm not so sure I should continue to relax and go with the flow. But even through my unease, I want to trust him.

Chapter 5

Tate

Joy is fucking gorgeous. And fun. I can't remember the last time I went out and spent most of the night on the dance floor. The second Gray and I walked into the bar, it felt like everyone stopped to stare at us like they'd never seen two cowboys walk into a bar before. Everyone except Joy and Rayna. As soon as I spotted her in the middle of the dance floor, it was painfully obvious that I wasn't the only man who noticed her. So, I did the only thing I could. I danced with her.

"You sure I can trust you to drive me home?" she asks as we reach my truck.

She's teasing, but there's uncertainty in her eyes. The thought of making her nervous sends a sharp pain through my chest. We just met, and she shouldn't trust me. But I want her to.

"Have I been anything short of a gentleman tonight?" I ask.

I open her door and help her step up, then rest my arm on the open door as I wait for her to respond. She looks up after fastening her seatbelt and seems surprised that I'm still standing here.

"Well?" I prompt.

Her large brown eyes look me over and I find myself shifting uncomfortably under her gaze. I adjust my stance so I'm not caging her in. Placing one foot on the running board, I rest my arm across my knee.

"What happened to your hand?" she asks softly.

I look down at it. It's a little bruised, but not too bad. I'm actually surprised that she noticed unless she saw the bandage in the parking lot. But I'm more surprised she hasn't already heard all about my fight with Grayson. Everyone else in the world seemed to know before I even made it to the doctor to have my hand looked at.

"It's nothing. And don't think I didn't notice the subject change. You comfortable giving me your address so I can take you home now?"

She offers me a polite nod, and I'm sure it's all I'm going to get, so I close her door and make my way over to the driver's side. I recognize the street name she gives me, so I pull out of the parking lot.

"You live down the street from Wyatt and Rayna?"

"Yeah. Next door actually, so no funny business."

I snort out a laugh. I've been trying to figure her out all evening. She was the picture of fun, buying drinks and dancing to almost every song. I don't know how to explain it, but that wasn't what drew me to her. It also wasn't the way she yelled at me for hitting her car. It was the hint of something beneath the surface. Something I get the feeling not everyone gets to see.

"No funny business," I agree. "I didn't realize you lived next to Wyatt. But I still would have volunteered to drive you."

"Oh? Why?"

Once again, she's analyzing me. I can feel it. The alcohol hasn't knocked down all her walls, not that I would take advantage if it had. I decide to use a play from her book and change the subject. She doesn't need to know that I just wanted a few minutes alone with her.

"Grayson and I got into it this morning. We don't really get along," I say, breaking the silence as I head down the dark country road. "You asked about my hand..."

Now it's her turn to laugh. "Yeah, I've heard you two don't get along."

"You heard that, but not about our screaming match that ended in me nearly breaking my hand on his jaw?"

Her eyes are wide as she looks from my eyes to my hand resting on the center console. She's so goddamn pretty I wish I could stare at her instead of at the road. It's dark, but I can still make out the shape of her eyes, her perfect nose, and the lips I've been doing my damnedest not to kiss all night.

Returning my attention to the road, I begin questioning my sanity. I volunteered to go out of my way to take her home, but of course, it isn't going the way I hoped. I've done something to fuck things up, and I have no idea what. I let out a startled gasp when I feel her fingers brush against my hand.

"Sorry," she says quickly.

"No need to apologize, sweetheart. I just wasn't expecting your touch."

She returns her fingers to the back of my hand, gently stroking and inspecting the best she can in the dark. It's a simple touch. It isn't suggestive, or sexual in any way. It's just my hand. But the unhealthy things my heart is doing in my chest would suggest otherwise. I let out a ragged breath as I allow her touch to soothe me.

"Did I upset you?" she asks after another long moment. "You almost seemed on edge when you suggested it was time to go."

"What?" I glance at her before looking back at the road. "No. It's just been a long, shitty day and I wanted to get you home before I gave in to my thoughts."

"What thoughts?"

I don't answer right away. We're on her street, and I'd rather look at her when I answer that question. Plus, I need a minute to decide just how much I want to say. I pull into her driveway, put my truck in park, and then turn to face her.

"That getting lost in you is exactly what I need after a long, shitty day."

She opens her mouth to speak then closes it without a word. Her hand is resting on mine, and I find myself terrified she'll move it. Now that I've experienced her touch, I need it. It's not the same as when we were dancing. That was fun. Casual. The way she carefully caressed my hand is personal. And at complete odds with our first interaction.

"I'm glad I didn't have to ride tonight because I've been completely distracted since I met you earlier. It's completely ridiculous, I know. Trust me, I know. I didn't expect to see you at the ranch, and I sure as hell didn't expect to find you at the Thirsty Pony."

I don't give her a chance to respond before I climb out of my truck and make my way over to her door to open it, holding my good hand out for her to take. She finally does, and I swear I feel a jolt of electricity. I don't miss her sharp intake of air. She felt it too.

"I'm sorry." Her quiet apology slices through the silence as we step onto her small porch.

"What are you sorry for?"

She lets out an embarrassed laugh before looking up at me, shaking her head. "I have no idea. Just felt like I should be sorry for something."

She's too damn cute. I laugh quietly before tucking a stray curl behind her ear. "You don't have anything to apologize for. If anything, it's me who should be saying sorry."

"For?"

"For spending the entire night thinking about kissing you. And for being a grumpy asshole because of it."

She reaches out and touches my hand again. The pain meds are beginning to wear off, and I wince slightly at her touch. She peeks up at me through her lashes and strokes my forearm instead, avoiding my battered hand.

"Fuck it," I mumble to myself before closing the distance between us and covering her lips with mine.

She stiffens briefly before relaxing against me as I wrap my arms around her, pulling her close. I take it slow, doing my best to feel her body's reaction. I don't want to be too forward, but I couldn't go another minute without tasting her.

Melting into my kiss, she lets out a sigh and I take advantage, sliding my tongue along the seam of her lips, silently asking permission. Her tongue meets mine and I finally allow myself to get lost in the kiss. To get lost in her. She tastes like lemons and sunshine. Like something way too fucking good to be mine.

Chapter 6

Joy

If I ever see another shot of vodka, it'll be too soon. Not because I have a hangover, but because I'm so damn tired. I spent the evening with Tate Garrison. Tate fucking Garrison. And he was nothing like the man I assumed he was based on our first meeting. He's kind. Polite. Caring. He's everything a cowboy should be. At least the cowboys in my mind, anyway.

The shower has done nothing to wake me up. I can't even remember the last time I went out and danced like that. It was probably when I was in my twenties, in which case I'm certain it didn't take this long to recover after staying up too late. But, *oh my god*, why did it have to be Tate Garrison who had occupied my time most of the night? There's no doubt he picks up women all the time. Women who know what a man like Tate expects.

I've been working at Boulder Ranch for months and have never laid eyes on the man. I'm not sure why I'm allowing myself to get so stressed out this early in the morning. Stepping into my boots, I head outside to Rayna's car. Mine is still at the Thirsty Pony, and even if I did have Tate's number, there's no way in hell I'd be calling him for a ride. I'm too old for any version of the walk of shame, so no matter what, I would be finding my own way to my car.

"So," Rayna says, waggling her eyebrows as soon as I get in beside her. "Tate Garrison, huh?"

I let out a groan. It would be nice to ride to work in peace, but I know she's dying for details. Especially since she has to drive me back to where I'm still parked. At the Thirsty Pony. I wouldn't be surprised if she's suddenly taken an interest in roughstock events.

"What about him? We danced. He drove me home."

"I know you're lying." She stops to laugh. "I watched the way you two were looking at each other. That's why I was surprised you needed a ride to your car."

I cross my arms and do my best to glare at her. "Really? Your horse is awfully high considering I only live here because of your vacation fling."

Her laughter fills the car as she pulls out of the driveway. I'm looking forward to working at the ranch, and it's not just because I love my job. It's the anticipation of seeing Tate Garrison on the back of a bucking bronco. I nearly fan myself just thinking about it.

Rayna raises a sculpted brow when I finally snap out of my fantasy and look her way. "So, you're telling me I was imagining all of that? The way he stared at you like you were the last slice of pizza?"

"I have no idea what you're talking about. We had a good time. Talked. He told me what happened to his hand. He wasn't looking at me like anything."

"If you say so. I'll see you later. Wyatt's off in the woods and I want to see for myself what those Garrison boys can do," she says as she pulls up beside my car.

I give her a quick thanks and then nod. Of course she wants to watch them ride. More like she wants to watch me. Boulder Ranch is only a mile or so down the road from the bar. Not nearly far enough away for me to get my head together before I have to face people.

By the time I get to work mucking stalls, I've finally stopped looking for Tate. I hadn't seen him before last night so there's no reason I should expect to see him now. Officially getting on my own nerves, I pop in my earbuds and start singing to myself as I work to drown out my stupid thoughts. I met a new person, danced, and had fun. The end. I'm not some thirteen-year-old girl who has a crush on every boy who's nice to her.

A firm grip on my shoulder nearly causes me to shriek loud enough to spook the horses. With a death grip on my shovel,

I whip around to see who's trying to give me a heart attack. I find Tate Garrison smiling at me with his hands raised. His smile is—wow—it's breathtaking.

"I didn't mean to scare you," he says with a low chuckle. "I called your name, but you didn't hear me."

I can't believe I missed the opportunity to hear my name on his lips. Stupid fucking earbuds. And stupid me for continuing to behave like I've never spoken to a man before.

"Sorry. Did you need me to do something for you?" I hate the way that sounds.

"No." His smile widens. "There's nothing I need that I can't handle myself. I'm over here to see you."

I'm pretty sure my brain has just shorted out. He's smiling down at me with those damn dimples. And the short beard I'd like to feel—nope. I will not let my mind go there. It's obvious he's here for a reason. The quicker he gets to it, the faster I can get back to trying to forget about him.

"To see me for what, if you don't need anything?"

"Oh, I need something, alright. I just don't need *help* with anything."

Despite my best efforts, I laugh. We shared a kiss last night, but I never thought I'd be standing here flirting with Tate Garrison. I lean my shovel against the wall and cross my arms.

"Semantics. What do you need, sir?"

He takes in a sharp breath before swallowing hard. *Good to know.* No. It is not *good to know*; what the hell is wrong with me? My face must betray my thoughts, because I look up to find him staring at me, his gaze dark.

"You didn't give me your number," he says as he passes his phone over with the contacts pulled up.

"I didn't know you wanted it."

His gaze darkens further as he once again swallows hard. "I thought I made myself pretty clear about wanting to see you again. Do I need to refresh your memory?"

My brows shoot up and I look around to make sure no one is near us. His question was vague, but it spoke straight to my core. I can practically feel his mouth on mine as last night replays in my mind.

"You don't want me to kiss you?" His voice is a low gravel, sending goosebumps over my body.

"Not when everyone can see us. I haven't worked here very long, and I don't want people to think I came to work here so I could pick up a cowboy or something."

He places his hand on the wall above my head and steps closer. "Who cares what people think? You going to watch me ride tonight?"

I pass his phone back to him. "If I'm not too busy."

Chapter 7

Tate

As soon as we line up to be introduced, I catch myself looking for Joy. And as my eyes scan the arena, taking extra time to linger around the gate that I found her leaning against yesterday, I can't help but notice she isn't there. I scan her spot by the gate one more time as I walk out. She is working. I know she's working. Yet here I am pining away like I'm not a thirty-eight-year-old man with more important things to worry about.

My hand isn't great, but it isn't broken and feels a hell of a lot better than it did yesterday. I flex and relax it, shaking it a few times for good measure. The swelling is way down, so I'm sure by the time I get out there, I won't be thinking about the pain; only about holding on for those eight long seconds.

"Looking for somebody?"

Looking up, I immediately make eye contact with Hayden Scott. He's been around the ranch for years in various roles, but the last few years he's been a bronc rider alongside me.

The competition is friendly, and I consider him a friend. Of course, he catches me very obviously looking for the woman who's been on my mind since last night.

"Nope. Just seeing how packed the arena is."

He doesn't even pretend to believe me, giving a dramatic eye roll and extremely obnoxious snort. I can't blame him. I wouldn't believe me either. I'm not sure what my problem is. I spent a few hours with the woman, and already I'm searching for her like she's someone important to me. I've had brief relationships. I know how things work. That's why I'm single. It takes much more than a few hours with someone to know if they're right or not. Hell, sometimes it takes more than a few years before you even get to know someone. I learned that the hard way from people I thought I could trust as close friends, only to find out I didn't know them as well as I thought I did. There's no excuse for me to be over here obsessing over a woman I met one time. Technically it was three times if I include both backing into her car and hunting her down like a stalker in the barn.

"It doesn't matter how crowded the stands are, it'll just be more people watching me kick your ass out there," Hayden teases.

I roll my eyes. I'm not cocky, but even if he does manage to get a better score, I highly doubt my ass will be kicked. Falling into step beside him, we walk out of the arena to find out our riding order. It's the start of a new season, so the order is as random as the horse we draw. I chance one final look toward the gate in hopes of laying eyes on Joy. But she isn't there.

I'm riding fourth. So far, Hayden is the only one who's managed to hold on for eight seconds. He did alright, but his horse didn't get the highest points. Mine, on the other hand, is a rough one. If I can manage to stay on, which I'm sure I will, I should have no problem beating Hayden's score.

I make my way into the chute, where my horse is already less than thrilled as he waits. Gingerly, I ease myself onto his back, holding on tight as he bucks and moves beneath me. As many times as I've done this, the nerves never quite go away. Several measured breaths are enough to put me into the right headspace. Focusing on my horse, I do what I can to match his energy. We want them to buck and do what they can to throw us off, but the style points come from making certain movements in time with the horse. Moving with them instead of against them.

My hand aches as I hold on tightly to the rigging. Next time Grayson stomps all over my last nerve, I need to remember to use my non-dominant hand to crack his jaw. My gloved hand holds on tight as I nod my head, signaling that I'm ready. With a loud clank, the chute opens, and my horse comes barreling out, bucking and turning. I grip tighter, even as I encourage the horse to try harder to get me off his back. My left arm remains up, and he tosses me around like I weigh nothing. With my thigh muscles burning, I work hard to stay in the saddle. Each buck of the horse sends me airborne before my body crashes back down onto the muscular animal. As soon as the buzzer sounds, the pickup men are beside me, helping me off the bronc and to safety.

When my boots hit the ground, I remove my hat, holding it up as I raise my arms to the crowd, celebrating another successful ride. The points haven't been tallied yet, but I made it eight seconds without being thrown off. After a few short moments, I return my hat to my head and struggle not to limp from the arena. This time when I glance at the gate, Joy and her friend are both leaning against it, watching intently. With a shy smile, she returns my nod as I make my way out of the arena.

Hayden pats me on the back as I walk past him. My score is a few points higher than his, but he isn't upset. It may be every man for himself, but it's a friendly competition. I'm not going out to be a world champion or anything like that. It's more like competing against the horses and other livestock. There's enough time between this ride and my next one that I don't even hesitate to make my way over to find Joy.

She seems slightly surprised when I saunter up to her, but there's no mistaking the smile that spreads across her full lips.

There's also no missing the nudge and encouraging nod Rayna gives her.

"You did pretty good out there, cowboy," she says in greeting.

"I'm glad you weren't busy."

She laughs, knowing I'm teasing her. I have no idea what to say, so I stand beside her and watch the next rider. Luke manages to stay on until the buzzer, and the crowd goes wild. Even though I'm standing there watching, I'm paying more attention to Joy and her excitement. Gene, the rodeo clown, goes into his routine after the last rider finishes up, so I turn to face Joy.

"You going out tonight?" I ask her.

"I don't think so," she answers with a laugh. "I'm still tired from last night. Are you?"

My lips pull into a smile. "I wasn't planning on it, and was crossing my fingers you'd say no so I didn't end up going."

Her smile is shy before she casts her gaze down. I'm getting the feeling the party-girl version of her wasn't quite accurate. Even better, as far as I'm concerned. I go out to the Thirsty Pony on opening night and sometimes after I ride, but I'm not much of a partier. My usual spot at the bar is either on the far end or off in the corner where it isn't packed. A drink or two with the guys and then I'm ready to get home.

"So did you leave a family ranch before you moved here to Cole County?"

She seems surprised by my question, cocking her head to the side before she responds. "How do you know I'm not from here?"

I have to laugh at that. Anyone who's spent more than five seconds in a small town should already know the answer. Everyone knows everything about everyone else. Or at least they think they do. And if there's one thing that gets people talking, it's a new face.

"You don't actually need me to answer that, do you? But I watched you with the horses, and you seem right at home with them."

She laughs along with me. "No. I guess I shouldn't be surprised that you know I'm new around here. I didn't grow up on a ranch, but my aunt has horses. She owns a facility that boards and trains horses. I spent pretty much every summer helping. When I was little it was to give my parents a break. But I kept going even as I got older and had a choice. It's hard work, caring for them, but it's peaceful."

I can't take my eyes off her. She has that wistful expression on her face that every horse owner gets, and I find myself leaning closer. I need to know everything there is to know about Joy Anderson. She fixes her ponytail and then returns her attention to me.

"Go to many rodeos back where you're from?"

She laughs again, and I know I'm grinning back like an idiot. "No. Actually, I've never been to a rodeo. We had a few girls who were barrel racers, but that's as close as I've been to any of this."

"Well? What do you think of it so far?" I glance toward the chutes where the first bull is getting ready.

"I love it. It's so exciting. And I love that I get to be behind the scenes. Do you still get excited? Is it just because it's new to me?" Her eyes sparkle as she looks up at me.

"The day I don't feel any excitement is the day I give up bronc riding."

She looks as though she wants to say something, but we're interrupted by the first bull rider. As soon as his introduction begins, the crowd is already going crazy. Joy has never seen professional bull riding before, so I know she's probably already forgotten I'm standing here.

"Hey," she says after I've turned to head back. The first rider barely makes it out of the gate before getting thrown off. "How's your hand? You didn't look like you were struggling out there."

Looking down, I flex and relax my hand, testing it out. "It seems okay. It did what I needed it to do so far. And it was fine when I went out to feed this morning. I've suffered worse."

"Do you have a ranch?"

I scoff at her, slightly offended that she would think otherwise. Of course I have a ranch. Does she think I look like a man who only spends his weekends on a horse? I look down at myself, trying to see what she sees.

"Yeah. I have over a hundred acres. Lived there my whole life. When my dad passed, it was left to me. I could show you one day. If you want."

"Yeah. I think I would like that."

"Well," I begin, sparing a glance at the chute where the next bull rider is getting ready, "I better get back there. I'm sure I'll see you around."

I feel her eyes on me as I make my way back to the other side of the arena. Grayson has to be coming up, and I still need to see him before he rides. That's the one thing I don't waver on. Doesn't matter if we're fighting, just finished beating the shit out of each other, or are on good terms, I'll never let him get on the back of a bull without saying a few words to him. He may know how to piss me the fuck off, but he's still my brother.

Chapter 8

Joy

Not to be dramatic or anything, but Mondays are stupid. Aside from Monday representing the official end of the weekend, I have to work my real job after being away for three days. As much as I enjoy helping people, I'd much rather hang out with the horses.

I haven't heard from Tate since Saturday and that's only adding to my shitty mood. He never said he would call, but the way he marched into the barn demanding my number, I kind of expected to hear from him sooner rather than later. I stare at the coffee pot as I wait for it to brew enough coffee to fill my giant travel cup. The way I'm feeling, I'll need every last drop.

Rayna is already at the front desk when I walk in. "Hey, girl. Did you save a horse yesterday?"

I stare at her in confusion. "I have no idea what you're talking about. Give me at least another few minutes for my coffee to kick in."

"Oh, come on. You know. Save a horse, ride a cowboy."

I roll my eyes. "I haven't ridden any horses *or* cowboys. I was off yesterday. Sunday is the day of rest."

Rayna cackles as she types something into the computer. "There are donuts in the break room. And coffee, in case you get through that gallon."

I walk past her and toward the breakroom so I can put my lunch in the fridge and grab my sweatshirt from my locker. The weather outside is mild, but they like to keep the office set to arctic. I feel sorry for any patients who have to get undressed in here. Emerging a few minutes later, coffee cup in one hand and donut in my mouth, I shrug my sweatshirt on.

"You really didn't see him? He didn't call you?" Rayna demands.

I blink at her as if I have no clue what she's talking about. She's talking about Tate. I'm not stupid. If I pretend like I don't know who she's talking about and like I didn't spend the previous day hoping my phone would ring, maybe she'll leave it alone. The only thing that makes coming to work less miserable is the hope that I'll be so busy, that I forget about stupid, sexy cowboys.

"The way he came to find you after his first ride had me certain he'd have found a reason to see you yesterday. What a dick. No worries, there are plenty more cowboys where he came from."

"Oh, my god," I groan giving another full-body eye roll. "I don't have a thing for cowboys. And I'm sure I'll see Tate around. Stop making this into a thing. It's not a thing."

The bells on the door jingle, drawing our attention to the entrance. Tate Garrison walks in and I immediately wish I was somewhere else. Anywhere else. His gaze meets mine, and it's like a magnet. I'm stuck staring into his eyes like a lost puppy. And not only do my eyes follow him, but I don't snap out of it until Rayna smacks my arm from across the counter. *Real fucking smooth.*

"Hi," I say in greeting. But it isn't a normal greeting. My voice comes out all breathy, betraying the emotions I'm trying my damnedest to hide.

"Hey." He looks directly at me as he walks the rest of the way to the front desk. "Dr. Robinson told me to just stop by sometime today to follow up with my hand. I hope this is a good time."

I swallow hard. "Oh. She, um... she didn't mention anything, but it's fine. You're the first one here, so no worries. Follow me." I nearly slap my hand over my mouth so I can shut the hell up.

It's first thing in the morning. I'm still half asleep because I only had a few sips of coffee during the short drive in. Wearing a pair of perfectly fitted Wranglers, a button-down shirt, and cowboy boots, Tate looks like he already won Monday. It takes everything in me to hide the spark of awareness I feel just being close enough to smell his earthy scent.

"So, how does your hand feel? Better than it did a few days ago?" I ask once we reach the room.

"Like I said, I've suffered worse. It's sore, but it'll be alright."

I reach for his hand to inspect it, doing my best to ignore the jolt my body feels when we touch. I'm a professional. I just need to take a quick look at his hand so I can do my job. As many times as I tell myself that, I can't stop thinking about the last time we were alone together. The way his lips felt on mine. The way he looked at me as though he was really seeing me.

"If you aren't comfortable with me touching you, just tell me, okay?"

He's watching me carefully when I finally look up to meet his gaze. "You can touch me anytime you want."

Jesus. There's no stopping my smile as I pump some hand sanitizing foam into my hands and rub it in. He's flirting with me. We spent an evening dancing and having fun. He drove me home and kissed me goodnight. I'm not sure why his flirting has thrown me so far off balance.

"Good to know." Once again, real fucking smooth.

"You're nervous," he says quietly, pointing out what I'm sure must be painfully obvious.

"I'm sorry. I'm not awake yet, and I didn't expect to see you. Also I didn't hear from you and... I don't know. I'm going to touch your hand now."

We're both quiet while I get to work checking his pulse while taking a quick look at his hand. My hands shake as I wrap the blood pressure cuff around his arm. I need to get a grip. I take a few measured breaths while recording his results.

"Okay, Dr. Robinson will be right with you." Turning on my heel, I make a beeline for the door.

"Wait." His deep voice stops me in my tracks. "I wanted to call you yesterday."

I remain frozen with one hand on the door handle as his words sink in. Finally, I turn around to face him, everything moving in slow motion as if I'm under water. He hasn't returned his hat to his head, so I have a clear look at his face. He's so good-looking, it hurts. He runs a hand through his hair, but the rogue locks flop back over his forehead as soon as he gives me a nod, confirming that I heard him correctly.

"Why didn't you?" I immediately regret the question, but I'm dying to know.

Shaking his head, he huffs out a laugh before looking down. When he looks back up, his eyes are serious, and they never leave mine. "I'm not sure. I convinced myself you wouldn't want to hear from me. I know how people talk in this town."

"What do they say?"

His smile is just wide enough for one dimple to show. "That I have a woman for every day of the week. That I'll never settle down. That I always leave the bar early but never alone."

I find myself stepping closer. "And that's not true?"

He's already shaking his head before I've finished the question. "No. Not most of it. And not anymore. Not many people know the real me, so I guess they just like to get creative when they come up with shit to fill in any holes."

"I'm sure people do that to me, too. I just haven't heard their versions yet. Anyway, I guess I'll see you around. I'll let the doctor know you're ready."

This time he reaches out and grabs my hand before I can walk away, and there's no ignoring the sharp breath we both take on contact. I look down to where his hand is grasping mine and then back up to his rich brown eyes. My mouth is completely dry as I swallow hard.

"I'd like to see you again, if that's alright. Are you free tonight?" he asks.

"I'm not busy, but I have to be at the ranch first thing in the morning to feed the horses and clean the stalls."

"Don't worry, I won't keep you too late. When's the last time you rode?"

"A horse?"

Once again, I want to smack my hand over my mouth, and his amused smirk only makes it worse. I'm not sure if it's nerves or excitement at this point, but I can't seem to get it together. I haven't been on a horse in years. I still make it a point to visit my aunt, but it isn't like when I was a teenager and would spend my entire summers and weekends riding and helping care for her horses. The thought of a ride has my heart racing with anticipation.

"Yes, a horse. But if there's something else you'd like to ride..."

"Oh, my god. I know you meant a horse, I just got excited. It's been a long time since I've gotten a chance to get on one."

"You should come by tonight. We can ride. I'll show you part of Cole County I'm sure you've never seen before."

Looking around the exam room, I try to find a reason to say no. I don't have to work. He was a perfect gentleman when he drove me home the other night, so I have no reason to be nervous around him; other than the fact that his very presence overwhelms me.

"I don't even know where you live."

"Drive like you're heading to Boulder Ranch but keep driving for another mile or so. I'm the next drive on the left. Five thirty?"

"Okay. Five thirty," I echo.

I leave the room in a daze, paying no attention to what I'm doing when I flip the plastic flag up signaling the patient in that room is ready. As I'm replaying the conversation for the twentieth time, I claim the empty seat beside Rayna.

"Why do you look like you've seen a ghost?" Rayna asks.

"I'm seeing Tate tonight," I breathe.

Rayna's eyes grow wide, and she spins the chair so she can face me. "As in, a date?"

"No. Maybe? Oh my gosh, I should have asked if it was a date!"

She holds out her hands and shakes her head, failing to hold in her laughter. "No. No you shouldn't have. Don't be weird. Tell me the plan, and I'll tell you if you should treat it like a date."

"He invited me to his place."

Somehow, her eyes get even wider. It sounds much worse when I say it out loud, and her reaction isn't helping me. I'm not even sure what's happening. Three days ago, he hit my car, and I thought he was a cocky asshole. Now, I'm planning to go to his house.

"That made it sound crazy. I think he invited me over to show me his land on horseback."

"You think?" Rayna has one eyebrow raised as she waits for me to explain.

"Yeah. He asked me how long it's been since I've been on a horse, then offered to show me part of Cole County that I've never seen."

"Well holy shit..."

Before she can say more, the exam room door opens, and heavy footfalls grow louder with each step. I turn in to see Tate walking in my direction... or in the direction of the door. Either way, I take the opportunity to look from his scuffed boots to the broken-in jeans, long-sleeved shirt, and finally his almost too-perfect face. Somehow, his beard looks both scruffy and neatly trimmed. His hat is back in place, with enough hair showing beneath to remind me it's long enough to run my fingers through.

When Tate's gaze meets mine, he tips his hat and flashes me a smile that nearly melts my panties. "I'll see you later, Joy."

And then he casually walks out the door, leaving me staring behind him. I'm going to need to give myself one hell of a pep talk if I'm going to survive the night. I've already spent time with him. I can do this. I know my way around a man. I'm Joy fucking Anderson.

"Yeah," I say, agreeing with Rayna's unspoken words. "He's crazy hot. Maybe I'll save a horse tonight."

Rayna's burst of laughter is exactly what I needed. Relaxed, I finally begin to look forward to the evening ahead. I didn't need a pep talk. I just needed a reminder of who I am. Even if I don't really intend to "save a horse" tonight.

Chapter 9

Tate

Pulling my phone from my back pocket, I glance at the time. Again. I clearly have no filter when it comes to Joy. Did I plan to invite her over? Absolutely not. I've got so much shit to catch up on around the ranch, the last thing I have time to do is entertain a guest. And not just any guest. The only person I've ever given a shit about impressing.

Glancing at the row of fencing that must be fixed, I hope I'll be finished before Joy gets here. At least I'm along the private road leading to my ranch so I'll be able to see her coming. I already had one steer get loose, I can't afford to have another one get out this close to the road.

Just as I'm finishing up the last section of fence that can't wait to be repaired, I hear the sound of tires crunching across gravel. She's here. The last section of fence will hold until I get to it. She slows as she reaches my truck, and I tip my hat before making my way over.

"You found me," I say as I pull off my gloves, tucking them into my back pocket. "Have any trouble?"

"Nope. Just like you told me, keep driving past Boulder Ranch and to the next private drive. I didn't realize you basically live next door to the place."

I give her a shrug. "Yeah. Our land borders, but I'd hardly call it neighbors when the only way I can really get there is using my truck or on horseback. I'm just finishing up, want to follow me up to the ranch?"

Smiling, she nods as she rolls up the window. I glance up at the gray clouds beginning to accumulate. It's supposed to rain tonight, but if we hurry, we should be back before the rain starts. Instead of leading her directly to the house, I pull into the gravel parking area beside the barn.

"It's supposed to rain later," I say as means of explanation. "We need to get started if we want to beat it. My plan was to get Cupcake ready for you, but the fences took longer than I expected."

"Awe, Cupcake is the one I get to ride?" she asks excitedly. "And I know how to tack up a horse."

I place a hand at the small of her back, leading her into the barn. I know she knows how to tack up, but in my head, I would have everything ready, and it would be like the perfect date of movies. It's hard to keep from laughing at how ridiculous my thoughts are getting. I show her where everything is, and she almost has Cupcake ready before I have my own horse set. Henry isn't exactly helpful as he spends the time trying to get to my pockets, in search of treats.

Once I lead Henry toward the trail that covers the perimeter of my property, he moves on auto pilot, setting an easy trot. Joy's smile is radiant when I glance over to check on her. Cupcake also knows the way and keeps in step. I haven't planned out anything I want to say to Joy, so I'm relieved when we fall into a comfortable silence. I point out landmarks as we pass, but she seems content to enjoy the ride.

"Your property is beautiful. It's so peaceful here," she says when we arrive at the pasture where the cattle are currently grazing.

"You like it?"

She turns to look at me, a genuine smile on her face. "I love it. Seriously, it's beautiful."

"Sometimes, if I'm having a bad day, I come out here to clear my head," I admit. "Out here it feels like there's no one else in the world. You can't see any houses. Can't see the road. Can't hear traffic. It's the perfect place to be alone."

"That sounds sad. And lonely."

"It's possible to be alone without being lonely." I look up and see the heavy clouds getting closer. "We'd better get back."

Shifting my weight, I take the reins, and Henry leads the way back to the ranch. The air is thick, warning of the impending rain. It isn't supposed to rain until much later, but I've been caught in shit weather enough times to know it won't hold off for much longer. The occasional raindrops hit my face as we make our way back at a steady cantor. As we get closer, the drops become more consistent, and I urge Henry to speed it up a bit, making sure Joy is okay when Cupcake follows suit.

We get back to the barn ahead of the rain, working quickly to untack the horses. It may have been a while since she's ridden, but she knows what she's doing. We brush them down, make sure they have plenty of water, then head outside. As soon as we get about halfway between the barn and the house, the sky opens up.

"Let's make a run for it!" I shout, reaching out to her.

Tugging her hand, I urge her past our vehicles and toward the ranch. The way it's raining, we'll only succeed in getting our seats wet if we try to drive over to the house. It's just as well we jog the distance. The rain is cold, but her touch is hot, nearly scorching my flesh as I tighten my grip. I'm trying my best to be a gentleman, but her white shirt is soaked through, revealing every curve. And her wet jeans cling to her thighs.

"Wait!" she shouts just before we reach the porch.

Joy leans against me as she pulls her boot off and tips it upside-down, doing her best to shake something out of it. She loses her balance a bit and steps her sock-clad foot into the muddy driveway.

"I thought I felt something in my shoe," she explains.

"Well, now there will be about ten pounds of mud as soon as you put that boot back on."

She's struggling to keep her balance in her haste to replace her boot, and I can't hold in my laugh. She's fucking adorable. Finally, she gets her foot back in and moves to continue our run for the house. I reach out and stop her before she can get too far or lose her shoe again. We're both soaking wet from the rain, and all I can think about is getting my mouth on hers.

"Might as well slow down, you're already soaked."

Chapter 10

Joy

The rain is cold as it falls over us, but I'm frozen in place looking up at the man towering over me. My hair is down, and I swipe at it, attempting to shove the wet curls out of my face, but it's no use. I must look a mess, but there's nothing but adoration in Tate's eyes as he continues to hold my gaze. He tucks a stray curl behind my ear before tenderly stroking my cheek with his thumb, causing my breathing to stop.

We've touched before, but this isn't the same. My skin tingles beneath his thumb and I close my eyes, leaning into the warmth of his touch. We're inches apart, but it isn't close enough. I want him to touch me.

"Can I kiss you," he asks as if hearing my thoughts.

I nod my head, afraid to speak. I don't want to break the spell we're under. Gravel crunches beneath his boots as he steps closer, and I feel the heat from his body moments before his lips crash to mine. There's no stopping the whimper that escapes my lips. The rain fades into the background as he uses the opportunity to deepen the kiss, swiping his tongue along mine as he pulls my body flush against his. The taste of the spring rain combines with the taste of *him*, and I'm sure I'll never get enough.

Desperate for more, I slide my hands up his arms and over his shoulders, tangling my fingers in the hair along the nape of his neck. His soft groan reverberates through me before he pulls back just enough to break the kiss.

"You're shivering," he says in a voice barely loud enough to be heard over the rain. "Let's get you inside and into some dry clothes."

Once again, I nod, accepting his offered hand as he leads me to the house. When I was in his arms, as his mouth worked over mine, I wasn't even aware of the cold. Now, I'm not sure if I'm shivering from the temperature, or from the way he makes me feel.

"The bathroom is to the left," he says, pointing to one of the closed doors. "I'll put some dry clothes in front of the door, and you can trade them for your wet ones so I can at least toss them in the dryer for you."

The flannel shirt he gave me to wear comes down to my knees, so I don't even bother with the way-too-big sweatpants. He also left me a towel so I could dry off after removing my wet clothing, and I hold it around myself with one hand as I emerge from the bathroom.

"Are you still cold?" he asks as soon as I step out. "I can turn on the heat."

"I'm much better now that I'm out of those wet clothes, thanks. The sweats were way too big, so I folded them and left them by the sink."

I swallow hard when I finally take a good look at him. He, too, is in dry clothing. Relaxed jeans, a black Henly, and bare feet. He looks so completely different from the other times I've seen him that I take a moment to look him up and down. His jaw is set as his gaze travels the length of my body, from my bare legs up to my wild curls.

"Your clothes should be dry in an hour or so. They were dripping wet. Would you like coffee or tea? Something stronger?"

"I'm easy. I'll have whatever you're having," I say, following him into the kitchen.

He opens the refrigerator and pulls out two bottles of beer. It isn't exactly what I had in mind, but I don't complain. Honestly, it doesn't matter; I'll take whatever liquid courage he wants to offer me.

"You hungry? I have chili on the stove."

I've been so thrown off by the unexpected rain, and the fact that I'm in Tate's house and not wearing pants, that I didn't even notice the smell of food cooking. I follow him over to the stove and try to sneak a peek as he opens the pot. Of course, I'm too short to see anything from behind him, but it smells delicious. My stomach growls, reminding me that all I've had to eat all day is the small lunch I packed for work.

"I'm starving," I admit. "And that smells amazing."

He removes two bowls from the cabinet, filling them both before passing one to me. "If you're warm enough, we can sit outside and listen to the rain. The patio out back is covered, and there's a fireplace. Plus, I keep blankets out there."

He leads me outside where there is an outdoor loveseat and two chairs. I sit on one end of the loveseat, assuming he didn't plan for us to sit on opposite ends of the patio and shout at each other as we eat. After setting his bowl on the end table, he makes his way over to the fireplace and gets it going before joining me.

The food is delicious, and we sit in comfortable silence, listening to the rain pattering atop the tin roof. It's comfortable, as if we've done this a hundred times. I didn't even realize how hungry I was until I started eating. I set my empty bowl down, slightly ashamed by how quickly I finished. He must catch my expression because he looks at me and winks as he sets his bowl beside mine. Fucking winks. I try my best to ignore what that tiny action does to my insides.

"So, what brings you to Cole County?" he asks, breaking the silence.

"That's kind of a long story." I'm not sure how much I should tell him. If he's making small talk, he certainly doesn't want to hear my life story.

"I've got all night."

I let a nervous laugh escape. "Well, it's not *that* long of a story, I guess. I just wasn't sure if you'd really want to hear it. Basically, I was stupid and allowed my heart to get broken, and Rayna convinced me to start over here since her office needed a part time medical assistant."

Tate watches me closely, clearly not impressed by my short version of the story. I can't remember the last time I went on a date, so I'm not sure what's proper date etiquette. I'm still not even sure if this is considered a date.

"I was in a relationship for nearly ten years. I thought it was serious, but he didn't. There's no real dramatic story behind it; he just wasn't feeling the same way. He had no interest in things becoming any more than what they were, and I'm too old to waste time on something that isn't going anywhere."

Tate is silent for several long moments, and I begin to worry I've said the wrong thing. It may have been a while since I've dated someone new, but even I know ex-boyfriend and girl-friend drama is not usually a good subject for first dates. But my story was literally drama-free. Then it hits me. I probably sound desperate as hell.

"I don't mean I'm on a hunt to get married or anything," I rush to explain. "Just that, I don't know..."

His face splits into a crooked grin. "You don't have to explain, I think I know what you mean. You want something that is going to progress. That's reasonable and doesn't sound desperate or anything, don't worry."

"You got so quiet; I thought maybe that came out wrong."

He shakes his head. "No, I was just listening to you."

I know I saw a change in him as soon as I said it, but I don't push. "What about you? What's your story?"

"It's kind of a long one." His lips curve into a teasing smile as he repeats my words back to me.

"I have all night."

He turns in the seat, bending a leg up and resting his arm across the back of the loveseat so he's facing me. "I kind of have to go back a ways for my story to make sense. I don't have much of one because the way life happened."

Placing a hand on his leg, I encourage him to go on. He swallows hard and takes a deep breath before continuing. The rain has increased, pelting the roof of the patio and drowning out what little background noise there is out here. I can't even hear the cattle in the distance.

"I used to ride bulls. I was out on the rodeo circuit before I turned eighteen and was pro for five years. I was the world finals event champion a few times before I quit at twenty-three. Then I've been running this place and looking after my brother, so I haven't had much time for anything."

I use one of his tactics and wait patiently for him to continue. I don't know Tate well, but I can plainly see there's more to it. Unless he has another brother besides Grayson, there are some major holes in his story. He brings up looking after him like he's not a grown man. I wait him out, but he's clearly better at this than I am. He's silent as I study his perfectly chiseled features, from his warm brown eyes to his square jaw. It's obvious he doesn't plan to elaborate, so I gently push him for more.

"Why did you quit if you were doing well on the circuit? And do you have a much younger brother? Where's he?" I didn't plan to fire off so many questions, but they kind of just spilled out once I started.

"It's just Grayson and me. Our dad passed when I was twenty-three and Gray was seventeen. So, I had to come back home and take over the ranch and look after him. I could have gone back out there, but as much as we argue and fight, I'm all he has. Our mom died when he was just a baby, so if something happens to me, he'll have no one. He may be thirty-two, but he still has a lot of growing up to do. I started bronc riding at

Boulder Ranch because I grew up riding there, it's right next door, and it's not as dangerous as bull riding. So, like I said, those things take up most of my time. I'm single. No ex-wives or dramatic ex-anythings."

My heart breaks for him, knowing what all he's been through. I can't imagine suffering a loss and then suddenly having to change my entire life. I'm fortunate that the worst thing I've had to deal with was the person I thought I'd spend forever with not feeling the same way. It broke my heart more than I'd let on to Tate, but it wasn't life altering.

"I'm sorry you went through all of that," I say quietly.

Giving me a sad smile, he shrugs his shoulders. "What can you do? It's been fifteen years, so it's just my life now. I don't know what I'd do with myself if I wasn't spending my time taking care of this ranch and trying to keep Gray out of trouble."

He makes it all sound like it's nothing, but I get the feeling it's just part of his tough exterior. I'm still not certain what tonight has been, but the more time I spend with Tate Garrison, the more I want to get to know what's beneath the surface. If I haven't ruined any chances of that by sounding like I'm hungry for a husband.

"Okay, well I should get going. I have to be at the ranch early in the morning. I had a really nice time, tonight." I move the blanket, revealing my bare legs and reminding myself I'm sitting here half-dressed. "You mind grabbing my clothes?"

"It's pretty nasty out, you sure you want to drive in this?"

I don't want to drive in this, and I don't really want to leave him. He's easy to be around, even after the obvious change in him when I explained my breakup. It's been so nice having a chance to relax and be myself. I don't regret moving here, but it's hard not to feel like the third wheel around Rayna and Wyatt.

"Yeah, I should go," I say gently.

"I'll get your clothes. Maybe we can do this again, without the rain."

I find myself smiling up at him, just as nervous as a schoolgirl. He's so damn sexy it hurts. And he's kind. He didn't tell me his whole life story, but it was enough for me to know the type of man he is. He's fiercely loyal and will do anything for the people he loves.

Chapter 11

Tate

It takes everything in me to keep from staring out the window as she drives away. I don't want her to leave. I'm fully aware of how insane and ridiculous it is to want to keep her with me, but I don't care. I feel better when she's around. I feel like it's finally okay to be my true self. There's no hero worship or preconceived notions. She knows me for who I am, not who this town thinks I should be. If nothing else, it's refreshing. It's so exhausting trying to be everything to everyone.

I don't deserve her. Especially after she spelled out what she needs in a man. She deserves to have a man who will give her everything she needs. Who will marry her, and give her children, and a white picket fence. I don't have that to offer. My plate is already full, but it doesn't stop the urge to be selfish and take what I can anyway.

The sound of tires rolling across gravel interrupts my thoughts. Lo and behold, I look out the front door to see Joy's car pulling back in. Has she changed her mind? Does she feel the same? I don't bother trying to hide my excitement as I yank the door open and step out onto the front porch.

She steps out of the car and stares at me, standing there frozen as if the rain isn't pouring down. After a moment, she shakes her head and makes her way toward me on the porch.

"Hey." Her voice is all breathy and it speaks directly to places it shouldn't. "Is there another way out of here? Your drive is flooded."

I shake my head. "Not unless you want to take one of the horses."

"Would you mind driving me home?" she asks. "Your truck could probably make it; it isn't too bad."

Again, I shake my head. "I'm not trying to be a dick, but with the way the rain is still coming down, I don't want to get stranded without a way back. I have to be able to feed the animals first thing in the morning. You can stay here. I don't have the guest room made up, but you can take my bed while I take the couch."

She tugs her bottom lip between her teeth. "I'll call Rayna and see if maybe Wyatt can come get me. He drives a truck."

As much as I'd like to have her sleeping in my house, wearing my clothes, I can't argue. There's no reason for her not to leave if she can get a ride. Honestly, if it came down to it and she really had to go, I would probably risk having to hike up my long ass drive to get back here.

"At least come inside so we can figure it out. You're all wet again and it's not getting any warmer."

I turn to head into the house, and she follows me even while pulling out her phone. Heading back to the linen closet, I grab her a towel while she makes a call.

"Hey, Rayna, can you have Wyatt come get me? Tate's road is flooded. My car can't get through, and Tate is worried if he leaves, he won't be able to get back to his animals if the rain keeps up."

I can only hear one side of the conversation as I make my way back, wrapping her in a fluffy gray bath towel. She places her phone on speaker, freeing up her hands to hold the towel around herself.

Rayna's voice fills the silence. "Wyatt's still off in the woods until tomorrow night. Why don't you see if Grayson can pick you up? I don't think he lives too far, and he drives a truck and obviously knows how to get to Tate's."

The very suggestion pisses me off. For what reason, I don't know, and I don't really care. All I know is absolutely the fuck not. I don't care if he's fucking River, or all of Cole County, he's not driving Joy home.

Reaching across the coffee table, I hit the mute button on her phone. "No. Just stay here. I'll throw your clothes in the wash and drive you to the ranch tomorrow. Honestly, if it's that important that you leave, then I'm willing to risk taking you home."

She looks at me, her face, a mask of indecision. After a long hesitation, she unmutes her phone. "Okay, Rayna. I'll figure something out. If anything, I can just get his number from Tate."

When the phone disconnects, she remains where she is, studying me closely. "You really don't want your brother to drive me home."

She isn't asking. "I'd rather he didn't. We got into it again before his ride because I walked in on him and River in the med room, and it was a whole thing."

Her lips quirk up into a small smile. "And your hand is okay?"

I laugh in spite of myself, and begin to relax. Keeping quiet, I wait for her to come to a decision. I really don't want to push her to stay here if she's uncomfortable and I also really don't want to drive her out to her place and then get stuck. I could stay at the Millers' if I can't get back down my driveway, but it's not ideal. Her resolve begins to crumble before my eyes.

"I have to work at the ranch early in the morning..."

"Yeah." I nod slowly. "I live on a ranch. I'm up early every morning. And I have to be there anyway. If the water hasn't gone down by morning, I'll drive you."

Slowly, she nods her head. "Okay."

"I'm sorry I don't have a spare room made up, but the sheets are clean. I'll grab you something to sleep in and then I'll take the couch."

It's already getting late, and I know she's been worried about getting up early so I don't want to drag anything out. And I want her to be comfortable. Lightning flashes in the distance followed by a low rumble of thunder as we make our way to my bedroom.

"Here." I pass her a T-shirt and a pair of my boxer briefs.

The sweats were way too big for her, but I'm sure she doesn't want to be completely bare while sleeping in a strange house with a man she barely knows. What the hell was I thinking, convincing her to stay here?

"There are fresh towels in my bathroom if you want a shower." I tip my head in the direction of the en suite. "If you need anything, I'll be in the living room."

I reach into my drawer and remove a fresh shirt and a pair of flannel pajama pants before leaving her alone in my bedroom. Once again, I'm wondering what the fuck is wrong with me.

My sanity is still in question as I go to the main linen closet, removing a sheet and a blanket so I can sleep on the uncomfortable sofa. It's not so much that the sofa is uncomfortable, it's that I'm six-foot-five. There is no couch that is comfortable for me to sleep on unless it folds out. And even then, there's a strong possibility my feet hang off.

I forgot to grab a pillow, but I'm not going to knock on the door to bother Joy for something that stupid, especially since I'm quite certain I will not be getting any sleep anyway. Not when there's a gorgeous woman mere feet away. A gorgeous woman who will be wearing my clothes and sleeping in my bed.

Chapter 12

Joy

It feels like hours that I've been lying here, trying not to think of the man on the other side of this door. But it's damn near impossible when I'm wearing his clothes and sleeping in his bed. The room carries his scent even more than the rest of the house, and I keep catching myself sniffing the pillow like a damn weirdo. This isn't the first time I've slept over at a man's house who I didn't know very well, but it's the first time I'm in a room all alone. I will my body to relax so I can at least get some sleep, or else tomorrow is going to be a long fucking day.

I jolt awake to find it's still pitch black, aside from the soft light coming from the bathroom. I couldn't have been asleep for more than half an hour. It must be because I'm in a strange place. I toss the blankets aside and swing my legs over, stepping onto the cold hardwood floor.

A glass of water might help. Slowly, I open the door and peer out. The rest of the house is dark too, the only light coming from above the stove in the kitchen. The ranch has an open floor plan, so I have a view of part of the kitchen from the hallway. The only thing between me and the kitchen is the large living room where I see the outline of the back of the couch where Tate must be sleeping. Stepping as softly as possible, I make my way to the kitchen. Rain taps against the roof, but it doesn't sound as heavy as it has been, so hopefully I'll be able to drive my own car to work. It's bad enough I've taken over the man's bedroom, I don't want him to have to drive me to work, too.

Chancing a glance at the sofa, it's impossible for me to make anything out besides nondescript lumps. I can't tell what's blankets and what's person. I don't want him to feel me staring at him, so I keep going.

"Couldn't sleep?"

My hand flies to my chest as my heart practically leaps from my ribcage. I nearly made it to the sink without even realizing Tate was in here as well. "Jesus Christ!"

"I'm sorry. Didn't mean to scare you." His voice is raspy either from sleep or lack thereof and I do my best to ignore my body's reaction.

Tate steps out of the shadows and joins me by the sink. He's shirtless in a pair of pajama pants that hang low on his hips. There's not enough light for me to make out the details, but I see enough to appreciate his muscular form. Enough to want to see more.

"I slept for a few minutes. I just came out for a glass of water."

Giving me a quick nod, he reaches into the cabinet and passes me a glass, his fingers brushing against mine as I take it. "Yeah, I couldn't sleep either."

He places his hands on his lower back and stretches while I fill my glass with cold water from the faucet. My eyes have somewhat adjusted to the dark, and I don't miss his slight grimace as he stands up straight.

"You okay?" I ask.

He gives me a nod but doesn't answer the question. "You hungry? I was just getting ready to heat something up."

"I could eat."

He takes a Tupperware container from the fridge and tosses it in the microwave before grabbing two forks from the drawer. I don't question him when he leads me to the couch a few minutes later with the two forks sticking out the top of the container of spaghetti. It's obvious once we get to the sofa that it is entirely too small for a man of his size. No wonder he couldn't sleep.

"Anything you want to watch?" he asks as he begins flipping through channels.

He briefly stops on a documentary I've seen before about a girl who is repeatedly abducted right in front of her parents, and they even know the guy who's doing it. I grab his leg and point at the screen. "Oh, my goodness! Have you seen this one? It's wild!"

Chuckling, he shoves a bite of spaghetti into his mouth. "Mmm hmm." He pauses to chew. "Most of it, anyway. You want to watch it?"

I nod eagerly, plucking a meatball from the container and popping it into my mouth. We share spaghetti and watch the documentary as if it's the most natural thing in the world. How we've fallen into a comfortable companionship is beyond me, but I refuse to overthink it. Earlier awkwardness aside, this is the first time I've felt like my old self since before I moved here. The breakup isn't on my mind, and I feel like there's no place I should be but here with this large cowboy who I barely know.

His hand finds my thigh, and the air in the room shifts. The only thing between his hand and my bare thigh is the blanket that's covering us. The touch isn't suggestive but tell that to the heat racing to my core. It's been a long time since I've experienced a man's touch, and just like during those stolen kisses, there's no stopping my body's reaction. I need his touch. Instead of being responsible and putting some distance between us, I cover his hand with mine. When I finally work up the nerve to steal a glance at Tate, I find him already looking down at me. His expression is unreadable in the dark, but I can feel his eyes on me.

I cast mine down and lower my head, taking in a sharp breath when he places his free hand along my jaw, tilting my head up before crushing his mouth to mine in a hungry kiss. Desperate for more, I kiss him back and part my lips to accept his tongue. Sparks zip across my body and my blood heats. His kiss is brutal. Feral. His hand slides into my hair, angling me the way he wants as he continues to claim my mouth.

Conscious thoughts drift away as I become a ball of sensation. This man kisses me exactly the way I need. He's demanding. Dominating. All-consuming. I slide my hands around his shoulders and pull him to me, feeling his corded muscles move and flex beneath my touch. I can feel it the moment his control snaps. His strong arms grip me tightly and he hauls me into his lap so I'm straddling him. He cradles my face with both hands as his tongue continues to explore my mouth.

I still can't get enough. His muscles are rigid beneath my greedy hands as I roam. I want to touch him everywhere. My core clenches as I imagine him with more than just his shirt off. He's hard beneath me as I grind against him, desperate for any sort of friction I can get. I've never been this turned on. I picture him filling me. Slamming into me over and over. It's obvious he's large just by what I can feel beneath his pants.

"Fuck, Joy," he grinds out.

Even the sound of his voice has my pussy clenching, desperate to be touched. I stutter out a breath. "Tate."

He shifts his weight and lowers me onto the sofa without removing his mouth from mine. His hands roam my body. Stroking and squeezing. Slipping a hand under my borrowed shirt, he strokes my skin and lets out a low groan when he reaches my naked breast.

"Please," I murmur, unsure what I'm even asking for.

I gasp and writhe beneath him when he teases my nipple. He doesn't stop until I'm trembling. My nerves are on fire, responding to every touch as his hand slides down, only stopping when he reaches the hem of my borrowed underwear.

"Please," I repeat. I want his hands on me.

Finally breaking the kiss, he pulls back to look at me. Everything stops as his warm brown eyes search mine. I could get lost in those eyes. They may be darkened by lust, but they tell me I can trust him. That he won't hurt me. I give a small nod and, finally, he slides his hand beneath the elastic waistband and grazes his fingers across my throbbing clit.

"You're soaked. Have you been waiting for me to touch you? Did you come out here looking for me?" His voice is a low growl, sending a shiver down my spine.

"No," I breathe.

"No?" His movements stop.

"I mean yes. I want you to touch me. But that's not why I came out here."

He resumes his movements; slow and leisurely. His fingers easily slide against my slick heat, drawing me nearer to the edge. I buck my hips, desperate to feel him. Desperate for release. Returning his mouth to mine, he swallows my cries as he slips two fingers into me while massaging my clit with his thumb. That's it. That pushes me over. My vision fades as wave after wave of pleasure shoots through me and my pussy pulses around his fingers.

"That's my girl," he breathes.

He places a kiss on my lips. My cheek. My neck. All the while he resumes his slow torturous movements across my sensitive slit while I continue to ride out my pleasure. The way he says those words is soft and gentle. Like he means them. Like I've given him something precious. It causes a warmth to spread across my chest as I lay there catching my breath.

"You should get to bed. You have work tomorrow," he says.

"But you didn't—"

"You should really get to bed." His voice is strained, and he lessens the sting by placing another soft kiss on my lips.

I hope it isn't regret causing him to send me off to bed. First of all, I'm an adult. And next, he is the one who initiated things. And those things were glorious.

I pull back but make no moves to get up. "Bed? Are you going to tuck me in?"

His smile looks sad as he shakes his head. "Not this time, sweetheart."

"Okay. Goodnight." I still make no moves to get up.

He lets out a short rumble of laughter before standing and pulling me to my feet. The sadness in his eyes combines with regret after he gives me another quick kiss. And then he sends me on my way, aroused and hoping there will be a next time.

Chapter 13

Joy

Somehow it feels as though I'm living through yet another Monday. The man beside me is consuming my every thought, but I've been trying to avoid him since I woke up. Unfortunately, I couldn't very well avoid him when I needed him to drive me to Boulder Ranch because the water is still too high. So, here I am sitting completely rigid in the passenger seat of his truck, terrified that he'll say something but desperate for him to do so.

"You okay?" His gruff voice pierces the silence.

"Yeah, I'm fine," I lie.

He spares the briefest glance in my direction before focusing on the rearview mirror as he backs up and turns around. I fell asleep as soon as my head hit the pillow despite my disappointment. But as soon as I woke up, I began replaying the events over and over. I was so turned on I wanted to beg Tate to fuck me. I felt how hard he was beneath me, so I know he'd been into it at some point. The only explanation for why he turned me down is that I did something to change his mind.

"Listen. Last night..."

He trails off and I use the pause to interrupt him. "It's fine. I was only still here because of the rain. Plus, I'm glad I didn't end up in your bed like all the other women. Well, to do something besides sleep."

"Other women?"

"Yeah. Come on, you're a legend around here. I'm sure you're quite... busy." God, I hate what a bitch I'm being. But he can't know how rejected I feel.

"No other woman has ever slept in my bed. Only you."

I'm certain I look like a fish out of water as I gape at him. "What? Certainly you've..." I gesture toward him, unwilling to finish that statement.

"I'm not saying I live like a monk. But I don't bring women home. Not on dates. And not for anything else."

Pulling into an empty spot in the gravel lot of Boulder Ranch, he directs his serious gaze at me. I can't look away. I need to get out of this truck before someone sees us. And I need to get away from him. He doesn't want me, and if I keep it up, I'm going to look like some pathetic fangirl. Even if he's never had another woman in his bed.

"Well, like I said, I was only still there because of the weather," I say quietly.

"And you were at my house because I wanted you there. Because I invited you."

He lets the meaning linger in the air. I'm trying hard not to over think this, because his reaction to me explaining my breakup would have me believing this man is far from looking for a relationship. So, this wasn't a date. And that's why he stopped things.

"Okay, well I'm going to be late." I reach for the door handle, but he holds up a hand to stop me before rushing to my side of the truck to open the door.

"I invited you to my house on a date. Because I wanted to spend time with you, and I wanted you to see a part of me that many people don't get to see. So, whatever this is, it's not something I normally do. Just so you know." He finishes speaking and steps aside, helping me to step out of the truck.

"Okay," I breathe. It's the only word I manage to form.

"What time do you get off?"

"You don't have to—"

He cuts me off. "What time do you get off?"

"Three."

"I'll be here." I watch as he walks away, leaving me standing here.

Shaking myself out of my trance, I make my way into the barn so I can get to work. The first thing I do is feed, so I make my way to the far end and work my way back. As soon as I reach the first stall, Miranda Wells rounds the corner.

"Hey, Joy. How's it going? Did you have a good night?" She pulls her light brown waves into a ponytail as she waits for me to respond.

"Yeah. I did have a good night. How about you?" Miranda and I get along, but her question is unusual. We usually talk about horses, and work. Every now and then we talk about local gossip. But we never talk about our personal lives.

She grins at me. "Something tells me my night wasn't as good as yours was."

I feign ignorance as I take care of the horse in the first stall, feeding him and making sure there's fresh water. Hopefully, if I get busy working, Miranda will take the hint and find something to do besides grill me. Usually, I feed all the horses then come back to muck the stalls. There are a lot of horses this time of year, and easily enough work to last all day. Even with more than one of us working. I look up to find Miranda still standing in the same spot, watching me expectantly.

"Don't look so nervous," she continues. "One could do much worse than Tate Garrison."

I allow myself a small chuckle. "Yeah. He is hot. But it's not what it looks like. I went over there so he could show me his land on horseback. I was saying it's been a long time since I've gotten to ride for fun. Anyway, we got caught in the rain and by the time my clothes were dry, his drive was too flooded for my little car to get through. And the water is still high, so here I am."

Miranda eyes me as if she isn't quite sure if she should believe me or not. I can't blame her. Honestly, if I had my way, there would be much more to the story than the version I gave her. If anything, the fact that he made it to at least—I don't know—second base, makes the fact we didn't have sex feel that much worse. That much more awkward. But he was pretty clear when he dropped me off that he's interested in *something*. I'm just not quite sure what.

"Well..." She trails off for several long moments. "Not to be a creep, but I watched the two of you before you made it into the barn, and something tells me riding horses isn't the only reason he invited you over there. Anyway, I won't keep you."

I'm left standing in the stall, gripping the railing as if my life depends on it. Tate came right out and said he invited me over to spend time with me. And that it's not something he normally does. And now I have Miranda saying she read all of that from our brief interaction outside of his truck. I get back to work, thankful I have an entire day to try and analyze everything. An entire workday before I have to climb into his truck and pretend like he hasn't changed everything in the course of a few days.

Chapter 14

Tate

It's been nearly a week since I've seen Joy and it's driving me fucking insane. I like to think we've left things on good terms, but as each day passes, I'm beginning to rethink that. We've texted back and forth a bit, but that's about it. No lengthy phone calls. No plans to meet up. The last I laid eyes on her, she was walking from my truck to her car before driving away, never looking back.

I'm sure it has everything to do with the way the night ended when she stayed at my house. Her body felt so good beneath mine, it took everything I had to keep from fucking her. My dick gets hard just thinking about how wet she was. And how responsive she was. I've had sex with my share of women, none of the relationships serious. Even though I'm not quite sure what I want with Joy, I know I don't want her to be like the others. As much as I tell myself I'm not looking for anything serious, I invited her to my house. And because of one night, it feels empty without her.

"Are you here to put in some work, or daydream?" Hayden asks as he reaches the gate.

A few of us decided to come by the ranch to get a few practice rides in. I've done what I can to help the other guys, but my heart just isn't in it. Hayden's right. I can't stop thinking about Joy, and what I need to say to her. I can't be upset about her halfway avoiding me, because it's my fault. The mixed signals I've sent are probably the biggest red flags. But how do I tell her I like her, only I don't have a fucking clue what I'm doing?

"Sorry, man. You're right. My head isn't in it," I admit.

"Feel like talking about it?"

I snort. "No. I mean—there isn't much to say."

Hayden adjusts his hat before folding his arms across his chest and pinning me with a look. We've been friends for a long time, but I've never been on this end of a conversation about women. As I told Joy, I don't have time for relationships. A fling here and there. A couple dates. That's all I typically bring to the table. But Joy makes me want more. She makes me wonder if maybe I *do* have time for more. Maybe I *can* have something that makes me happy.

"I kind of met someone," I say slowly. "And I think I was so busy trying to convince myself that I can't have her, that I ran her off."

"Okay, so Joy is mad at you. Have you called her? Stopped by the barn to tell her how you feel?"

"How do you know I'm talking about Joy?"

Hayden lets out a loud snort as he rolls his eyes. "Please. Everyone knows you're talking to Joy. And we all know you dropped her off here the other morning, so it was safe to assume things were going pretty well."

"Fucking small towns," I mutter under my breath. "That wasn't what it looked like. No wonder she's avoiding me. She got stranded at my house after the flash flooding. Her car couldn't get across the rising water. But we didn't sleep together or anything."

Once again, he stares at me and waits for me to continue. I can pretend like it's nothing all I want; Hayden knows me better than anyone. He knows I'm full of shit. Looking down, I move some stones around with the toe of my boot.

"Okay fine. Something got started, but I put a stop to it. I don't want her to be like the other women. That's why I invited her to my house instead of to the bar or out to dinner. I wanted to spend time getting to know her." Hayden stands beside me and leans his back against the gate, giving me his full attention. "She's not just some girl you hook up with, you know?"

"Does she know that's why you didn't fuck her?"

"Watch the way you say that," I snap. "And, yeah. I mean, she should. I told her I don't just invite women to my house."

His soft chuckle can barely be heard above everything going on in the background. "Okay here's my advice: explain to her why that night ended the way it did. Tell her exactly what you told me, and more. She can't read your mind."

"You make it sound easy. She's not exactly going out of her way to talk to me."

"Then you go out of *your* way. You ride horses that do everything they can to throw you off. You should be able to talk to a girl you like."

I scoff. "I'm not afraid to talk to her."

"Well then why haven't you?" he demands.

"Fuck off."

I don't say the words with my whole chest. He knows I don't mean it. Still, I turn to walk away before he can say anything else. He's right, though. I've been moping around for days, when all I have to do is either stop by the ranch or find her at the doctor's office. Hell, I could even stop by her house. I know where she lives. But I don't want to corner her and force her to talk to me.

"Isn't that her car over there?" Hayden nods in the direction of the parking lot where, sure enough, Joy's car is parked along the wooden fence.

"How the hell do you know which car is hers?" I demand.

"Like I said, it's a small town. She's hot and single and works here at the ranch. Of course I've noticed her enough to recognize her car."

I force myself to be silent before I say something I'll regret. No matter how much it pisses me the fuck off that he's been checking Joy out, I don't have any claim to her. She's not my girl.

"Quit being such a fucking baby and go talk to her."

I walk away in silence. No need to tell him he's right. I just need to stop being a fucking baby. I march over toward the barn before the quick pep talk wears off. *Quit being a fucking baby.*

Chapter 15

Joy

Of all days for Tate to find me in the barn, he chooses the worst possible one. I'm covered in shit. Literally. And on top of that, I'm a sweaty mess. It's been warm for the season, and it really doesn't take much to work up a sweat when taking care of horses and mucking stalls. As far as being covered in actual horse shit? That doesn't take much either.

"Tate, it's really not a good time," I say, praying he'll just leave.

If he didn't want me when I was freshly showered and wearing his clothes, I definitely don't need him to see me like this. He looks at me like I'm not a complete disaster and steps closer. I swear I wish I could disappear.

"If you really want me to leave, I will, but I need to talk to you. That's why I'm over here."

As sincere as he appears to be, I just can't have him this close to me when I smell like a barn. Like an actual barn. I'm surprised he came to find me. It's been days since our awkward ride back to his house to get my car. And then I've pretty much avoided him like the damn plague.

"Can we please do this another time?" I plead.

"Okay, when? I'm not doing anything later..."

I stare at him for a long moment before looking down at my feet until I can work up the courage to meet his gaze. "Tate, I'm filthy. I'm sweaty. Can you please just..." I trail off.

"Just what?" He steps closer as he asks, causing my heart to pick up speed with each of his movements.

"I don't know. I'm free tonight; but look at me. Tomorrow night is Saddle Club, and I work at the doctor's office during the day. How about this weekend?"

He's shaking his head before I even get the words out. "I'm traveling to an event this weekend. It's the only one I travel for."

Immediately, my mind goes to his unwillingness to drive me home when the water was rising. "I thought you couldn't be away from the ranch."

"Hayden always takes care of the animals for me since he doesn't travel for anything anymore. Like me, when he finished in the rodeo circuit, he started sticking around Boulder Ranch for the season. Just come over when you're done. You've showered at my place before."

And now my mind wants to replay that night, and how it ended. It sends my heart racing just thinking about it.

That's probably what he wants to talk about. Explain how it shouldn't have happened and could we just go back to being friendly acquaintances. Regardless of what he wants to talk about, I just need him to not be here.

"Will that get you out of here?"

A grin spreads across his face. "Yes."

"Fine! If you can't just wait or talk to me over the phone, then I'll come by after work."

Somehow, his grin goes wider before he tips his hat and walks away. Of course, I watch as he walks away because how could I not? I will not miss an opportunity to appreciate the way he fills those jeans out.

I get back to work, hoping more than anything that the last few hours will go by fast. From what he said when he dropped me off the morning after I slept at his house, I'd expected him to say more when he brought me back to my car. Maybe he would ask to see me again or tell me what his intentions were. Something. But instead, there was nothing. Hopefully we at the very least get things straightened out.

Once again, I find myself sitting on Tate Garrison's couch, wearing his clothes. And once again I'm at the mercy of the washer and dryer before I can go home. I'm grateful he didn't listen to me when I claimed he didn't need to wash my clothes. I can't imagine showering and then bringing those nasty clothes home.

"You want to decide what we watch again? You didn't do so bad last time."

I smile in response, but inside I'm going crazy waiting to hear what he needs to say in person. We could have kept the small talk for the phone. Looking up, I find his eyes already on me, waiting expectantly for my response.

"Are you going to torture me, or tell me what it is that couldn't wait for a better time?"

His lip tugs into a cocky smirk, and I want to shake him. The entire rest of my workday was spent trying to guess what he was going to say. As soon as I'd have myself convinced that whatever he had to say would be good, my brain would remind me how things usually work.

Crossing my arms, I turn away to look in the opposite direction. His hand grips the back of my neck and before I can react, he hauls me to him, stopping when we are mere inches apart. I sit frozen, staring into his warm brown eyes. His nearly shoulder-length hair falls forward without his hat to keep it in place. My breathing is coming in short gasps as my eyes dip to his lips in time to catch a glimpse of his tongue as he moistens them.

He parts his lips, but instead of speaking, he crashes his mouth to mine. His mouth is demanding, urgent as his tongue teases at the seam of mine. There's no stopping the soft moan that escapes as I open for him. Heat pools at my center when I recall the way his hands felt on me. I need him to touch me again. I need more. His grip on my waist is nearly painful as he holds me close.

"I could kiss you forever," he murmurs.

Too stunned to respond, I search his eyes. We're back to being mere inches apart, and I take a moment to brush his hair from his face. It really is ridiculous how good looking this man is.

"I'm sorry about all the mixed signals," he says before pausing to press a gentle kiss to my lips. "I don't know what I'm doing."

His mouth is warm as he places more kisses along my jaw and down my neck. I'm lost to the sensation of having him near me and showering me with his attention. His scent overwhelms me as he holds me close. Finally, his words register in my mind.

"I find it hard to believe you don't know what you're doing. There's no shortage of women who want you."

"Yeah, but none of them are you." His expression is serious as he studies me carefully.

Before I can ask him to explain, his mouth is back on mine. The kiss is urgent, but thorough. Keeping one hand along the side of my face, he holds me still while his tongue entwines with mine, tasting and exploring until I'm so filled with need, I can barely stand it. I'm trembling in his arms from the anticipation.

"None of them are you," he repeats. "I don't know what I'm doing because I've never wanted anyone like this. I want all of you. Every secret. Every fantasy. Every disappointment."

His mouth is back on mine as his hands begin their exploration. I'm wearing one of his T-shirts and a pair of his flannel pajama pants. No bra. No panties. I'm nothing but sensation as his hand slides up my body, over the shirt. He starts at the slight curve of my stomach and travels up until he reaches my breast. He lets out a whispered curse when the only thing separating him from the bare flesh of my breast is the thin T-shirt he lent me.

"I didn't want to stop things when you were here before. I wanted you so goddamn bad, but I didn't want you to be just someone I hooked up with. I've never had an interest in anything serious, so my date nights usually consisted of going to dinner and a movie; something generic and impersonal. I didn't want that for us. I wanted to spend time with you just getting to know you. And I wanted you to see this part of me that no one else sees. I didn't expect to nearly ditch all sense of self control."

I continue staring at him. I'm not sure if he's explaining why he wants me or trying to tell me we should stop. His hair has returned to his face, draping like a curtain along his cheek. I reach out to brush it back, but stop short, his words echoing in my head. I freeze in place, unsure if he wants me to touch him or to take a few steps back.

"Please," he whispers, his eyes pleading as they remain locked on mine. "Please touch me."

I rake my fingers through his hair in an attempt to remove it from his face, and he melts into my touch. His eyes are closed, and his lips parted. I don't think I've ever seen a more beautiful sight than when he rests his cheek against my outstretched hand.

"Your touch feels like heaven," he breathes.

Chapter 16

Tate

I'm not sure what this woman is doing to me, but whatever it is I hope she never stops. One touch from her and nothing else matters. All my responsibilities, everything I have planned—it all disappears. Her warm, brown eyes are filled with uncertainty and my chest cracks open as the last of my resolve finally crumbles away.

She came here so we can talk—and we will—but right now I need her. Moving slowly, I slide my hand beneath the hem of her shirt and stroke the warm, soft flesh of her stomach. Her breath catches, and I keep my eyes on her as I revel in the feel of her smooth skin beneath my hand.

"This is okay?" I ask in a low voice.

She nods her head, so I allow myself to explore, sliding my hand up to her breast and gently teasing her nipple. A gasp escapes her parted lips, the sound going straight to my already aching cock. Everything about this woman is perfect. Perfect and completely out of my league. Bracing myself above her, I lean forward and claim her mouth while my free hand continues greedily seeking every bit of naked flesh within reach.

Her body trembles beneath me as I continue to kiss her as if I need her mouth to survive. When she grips my belt and begins fumbling with the buckle, I pull back enough to let out a muffled curse. I should stop her; I know I should. Instead, I stand, my eyes glued to hers as I undo my belt and pull it free with one hand before tossing it aside. Her shocked expression makes me laugh as I undo the button on my jeans. Instead of removing them, I reach for my shirt and tug it over my head, tossing it before I return to the couch.

"I know I asked you to come here so we could talk." I reach for her and pull her onto my lap so she's straddling me. "But right now I need to touch you."

Instead of responding, she covers my lips with hers, her kiss telling me she feels the same way. She runs her soft hands over my chest, up to my shoulders, and finally slides a hand up the nape of my neck and into my hair. Fuck, her touch feels too good. I close my eyes as a tortured moan escapes me.

"I love your hands on me," I breathe.

Her breathing is heavy as she rakes her eyes over me, and she doesn't object when I grip her shirt and pull it over her head. *Holy shit.* She's so damn perfect. Her breasts are slightly more than a handful with pebbled nipples just begging for my touch. I lean forward, take one into my mouth, and flick the hardened peak with my tongue. She practically convulses on top of me and presses her heat against my throbbing length.

"Fuck, darlin'," I grit out. "I need to feel you. All of you."

"Yes," she whispers.

"Yes?" I repeat it as a question, making sure she means it.

She nods her head, holding my gaze. "Yes."

That single word is all I need to hear. "I want you out of those pants."

She clambers off me, clearly in a hurry to do as I asked. I keep my eyes on her as I unzip my jeans and shift on the seat so I can slide them off. Removing my wallet from the back pocket, I toss it onto the end table before discarding my jeans and opening my arms in invitation. Joy is gloriously naked. Her soft curves cause my mouth to water. I want to taste every last inch of her.

"No fucking panties?" I growl when she spreads her legs to straddle me once more, giving me a perfect view of her wet slit.

"They're in the wash with the rest of my clothes," she explains.

I grip her tight, holding her still while I once again claim her mouth in a hungry kiss. It doesn't take long before the kiss turns desperate, both of us needing more. She shoves her tongue into my mouth and tugs my hair as she angles me to fit against her. Fuck is that hot. I buck my hips, pressing my arousal against her warm center. The only barrier between us is my boxer briefs as she rocks against me.

I grab hold of her waist, stopping her movements. "This will be over before it gets started if you keep that up."

Reaching for my wallet, I pull out a condom, placing it between my teeth while I lift up and maneuver out of my briefs. Joy's eyes are wide when I look up to meet her gaze. I slide my hands up and down her thighs while I wait for her to say something.

Removing the condom from between my teeth, I hold it in one hand while I continue to caress her skin. "You okay?"

She glances down at my dick and then back up. "I just wasn't expecting... that."

Sliding my hand up her thigh, I graze her slit with my thumb. "Nervous?"

"Yes," she admits before tugging her bottom lip between her teeth.

I run two fingers along her slit, spreading her arousal over her clit and then tease along her entrance. The sounds she makes go straight to my cock. I want to bury myself in her. I want to claim her. But not before she's ready. She's soaking wet, easily taking my finger when I slip it inside.

"I won't hurt you," I say gently. "We'll take things slow."

I tear the condom wrapper open with my teeth, so I don't have to let her go. She watches me closely, eyes wide as I roll the condom over my hard length. My gaze collides with hers and I'm momentarily frozen as her eyes search mine. Running my hands over her soft skin, I continue to hold her gaze until I feel her begin to relax under my touch.

"You ready for me?" I ask.

She nods her head.

"Tell me," I demand, my voice less gentle than it was a moment ago.

"Yes. I'm ready. I need you." Her voice is a needy whimper.

I position her above my cock and slowly lower her, stopping when she takes the first inch. She's so tight. And wet. And warm. I want to bury myself the rest of the way inside her, but I force myself to slow down. My muscles are tense as I struggle to maintain my control.

"More," she whines.

With shaking hands, I slowly lower her the rest of the way down, and my vision nearly goes black from how good she feels. We both let out a low moan when I'm fully seated inside her, and I give her a moment to get used to the way I feel.

Her eyes snap open when I buck my hips hard enough to make her gasp. Her lust-filled eyes hold mine as I repeat the movement. Again. And again. My body takes over, chasing the release it so desperately needs. Her movements match mine and her grip on my hair tightens as I continue slamming into her.

Between the sinful sounds coming from her mouth, the way her pussy squeezes me, and the delicious burn from her tugging my hair, my balls are already tightening along with the familiar tingling down my spine.

"That's right, baby. Ride my cock," I grind out. "Take what you need."

She does take what she needs. Her grip on my shoulder tightens as she finds her rhythm. When her movements become erratic, I take over, slamming her down on my cock as my thumb finds her clit and presses, making slow circles until her body stiffens above me.

"Oh shit, I'm going to come," she breathes.

She barely gets the words out before she tips her head back and I feel her pussy pulse and squeeze my cock, drawing out my own orgasm. This time, my vision does go dark as pleasure races through me in waves. Every muscle in my body is tense as I continue to pulse inside her until I finally relax and sink back into the couch.

"Did I hurt you?" I ask after I've finally caught my breath enough to speak.

I feel her smile against my neck. "No."

I don't even know what to say. I don't want to move. I just want to stay here with Joy draped over me like a blanket. She winces when I remove myself and slide her from my lap so I can head to the bathroom to ditch the condom and get cleaned up, leaving her curled up on the couch.

I gently swipe the warm washcloth I brought back along the apex of her thighs to clean away the remnants of our lovemaking. "You sure I didn't hurt you?"

Her eyes remain closed, but a smile spreads across her face. "No, Tate. You didn't hurt me. That was... wow."

I toss the rag onto our pile of discarded clothing before pulling her into my arms. "Will you stay the night?"

"I have work tomorrow," she reminds me.

"Yeah, and I get up early for chores. I'll make sure you're up."

"Okay," she answers softly.

I can't tear my eyes away from her. She's beautiful. No makeup. Hair, a wild mess of curls. Her brown skin radiant beneath my rough hands. Pulling the blanket from the back of the couch, I cover her so I can get up before I change my mind.

"You stay here. I'll fix us something to eat."

I force myself to walk away when all I want to do is hold her. But more than that, I also need to take care of her, and that includes making sure she eats. Making sure she's warm enough. Making sure she's comfortable with me. Because one thing is certain: now that I've had her, I'm not letting her go.

Chapter 17

Joy

"Who the hell is planning a date for Monday night, anyway?" Rayna asks as I glance at my watch for what feels like the hundredth time.

I've been on edge ever since I walked in and glanced at the schedule of patients. The afternoon is booked solid, which almost always means we won't be getting out on time. But that's not the point. Even if I didn't have plans, there's literally nothing worse than getting out of work late. As a rule, we aren't supposed to have the schedule that full.

"That's not the point," I argue, cutting my eyes at my friend. "I'd want to get out on time even if I didn't have anything to do after work."

She laughs to herself as she types away on the computer. "Calm yourself, it'll be fine. We'll make sure you get out of here on time. What do you have planned for tonight?"

I shrug. "I don't know. The point is, I don't want to be stuck here."

Now, she's laughing, and as much as I want to be pissed at her, I can't help but laugh along. I'm being dramatic, but I haven't seen Tate since I stayed the night at his house. Our schedules didn't match up, and then he was out of town. This is his first day back. I know it's stupid and clingy, but I miss him.

"It looks like after Mr. Crawley's appointment there's a break until that madness after lunch. You want to order pizza?" I suggest.

Rayna looks surprised by my suggestion but recovers quickly. "No, I brought a salad, but you can see if Dr. Robinson wants something. You didn't bring a lunch?"

"I did, but I'm not hungry for a sandwich. If I have to deal with all of Cole County after lunch, I need my strength."

Rayna laughs and shakes her head. Before she can say anything, the bells chime as the door opens, and Mr. Crawley walks in. Pasting on a smile, I pick up my tablet and make my way around the desk. By the time I make it around, I become aware of the dog standing beside him.

"Mr. Crawley, you can't bring a dog in here." I point at the sign on the door.

"Patches isn't botherin' anybody. Now, come on. I have a twelve-thirty tee time, and you're gonna make me late."

I open my mouth to argue, but snap it shut without saying anything. I'd be surprised to find out Old Man Wilber golfs.

Even if he did have a tee time, there would be no way he could make it all the way to the other side of the county by twelve-thirty. Not even if he left right this second.

"Follow me," I say with a sigh and a raised eyebrow directed at the dog.

I take him into the last exam room. That way, if the dog makes a mess, it'll be easier to avoid the room until it's cleaned. The nurse is off, so I ask the regular intake questions as I take his vitals.

"So, what brings you in today?" I ask as I take his wrist and measure his pulse.

"The missus said I had to come in because I was sick last week," he answers in a gruff voice.

"Oh, okay. What seems to be bothering you today?" I ask as I enter his pulse rate into the chart.

"Nothing. I said I was sick last week."

My brow is furrowed as I wrap the blood pressure cuff around his arm and use the stethoscope to listen. I enter the perfect numbers into the chart. His vital signs are better than mine.

"So, nothing is bothering you?" I confirm.

"No. Like I said. Last week."

"Okay then," I say, doing everything I can to keep from laughing as I walk to the door. "The doctor will be with you in a minute."

As soon as I have the door open, Patches slips past me and takes off down the hallway. I curse under my breath as I take off after him. It's no use. The dog has to be as old as Old Man Wilber, but he moves like a damn puppy. He ran toward the reception desk, so I'm crossing my fingers that he's headed to Rayna.

I get to the desk and find Rayna leaning back in her chair scrolling on her phone. "Is Patches with you?"

She sits up in her seat and looks at me with wide eyes. "What do you mean, is he with me? You let the dog run loose? Dr. Robinson is going to be pissed."

"Why am I going to be pissed?"

"Oh, Rayna's just joking," I answer quickly. "Mr. Crawley is in room six."

Dr. Robinson pulls her reading glasses from the top of her head as she picks up her tablet and heads to the room. I hold my breath and cross everything as I watch her walk down the hallway toward the exam room. Where the hell could that dog disappear to? As soon as she closes the door of the exam room, I start checking every room, looking for a trace of Patches, but I see nothing. I don't even hear anything.

As soon as I finish checking the exam room closest to room six, I hear a crash followed by scrambling coming from the supply closet. I could have sworn the door was closed when I walked by, but low and behold, Patches comes tearing out of the barely open door with a mouth full of...

"Patches?" I whisper-shout. "Patches, what the hell do you have?"

Of course, he doesn't answer me. He shakes whatever it is, and droplets go flying before he takes off into a run, leaving a wet trail behind. I'm trying not to make a lot of noise, but as I gain on the rogue animal, he kicks into high gear and starts running circles around me. Tail wagging hard enough to shake his entire body, he sits in front of the door and watches me. It's an IV bag.

"Oh, my god," Rayna says slowly. Her lips are rolled, but it's obvious she's trying not to laugh.

I give Patches my fiercest glare as I reach out my hand and slowly approach. He gives the bag another shake, sending normal saline spraying, but he doesn't run. As soon as I get close enough, I lunge. Patches takes off right when I make my move, and instead of getting my hands on him, my foot lands in a small puddle and I go flying.

It isn't a graceful fall. It isn't a little slip. No, of course not. My feet go up in the air, and next thing I know, I'm flat on my back staring up at the ceiling as my vision returns to normal.

"Are you okay?" Rayna's footsteps get closer until I finally see her face peering down at me.

Closing my eyes, I take a cautious breath, groaning at how sore I already am. "Yeah. I'm okay. I just need a second."

Rayna kneels beside me, placing one hand on my shoulder and taking my opposite hand to help me sit up. I take a few more slow breaths and as I nod my head and grip her hand, I hear the bells on the door jingle as someone comes in. Because of course they do.

"Joy? What happened? Are you okay?" I turn my head at the sound of Tate's voice and scramble to sit up straight. "Hey, easy, now. Are you hurt?"

The concern etched into his features and the compassion in his voice are enough to cause my lip to quiver. I'm so embarrassed, all I want to do is disappear. As if falling flat on my ass isn't bad enough, Tate has to be present for my humiliation.

"I'm okay. I think I just got the wind knocked out of me."

Tate lowers himself to the floor and holds me against his chest as he runs his hands over my body. "You sure you aren't hurt? Maybe have Dr. Robinson take a look before we leave?"

"Before we leave? How long was I out? It's the end of the day?" My voice rises in panic with each word.

Tate's arms tighten around me, instantly helping to calm my nerves. "Hey, you're okay. It's lunchtime now. That's why I'm here. Rayna didn't tell you I was coming to pick you up at lunch?"

I whip my head in the direction of my friend's surprised giggle. She resembles a deer caught in headlights and slaps her hand over her mouth, muffling her laughter.

"I was going to, I swear. I just didn't get that far."

I glance at Tate and find him glaring at Rayna. "What do you mean you didn't get that far? I called first thing this morning to make sure it was still okay for her to take a half day."

"Oh, my heavens! What happened out here? Are you okay, Joy?" Dr. Robinson is clutching her chest as she rushes over to me, and I wish once more that I could either go back in time and not fall on my ass or disappear. Either one would work.

Tate helps me to my feet and directly across from me is an incredibly happy dog. Patches sits beside his owner, looking around as if he has no idea what all the commotion is about. Damn dog.

"I was chasing after this escape artist of a dog and slipped and fell. It's not a big deal, I'm fine. He got hold of an IV bag and made a mess. I'll get it cleaned up so no one else falls." I try to remove myself from Tate's grasp.

"You'll do no such thing. You have plans this afternoon. We'll take care of it. But why don't you let me make sure you're okay," Dr. Robinson says.

Clearly, everyone except for me knew about my plans. I want to be annoyed, but I love that Tate planned something for me and even went as far as to call my job and clear some time off. Or tried to clear some time off, anyway.

"I'm sorry, Tate. It's way too busy. Dr. Robinson, I can't leave you guys here with all these appointments."

"Um..." Rayna's voice is soft. Too soft. "There are only two appointments this afternoon. I was just messing with you. In my defense, I didn't expect for all hell to break loose before I could tell you it was a joke. You were supposed to come back to the desk, mention lunch again, and I was going to tell you something funny about having Tate for lunch."

"Okay then!" I say far too loudly just to stop Rayna from saying anything else. "I'm just going to grab my purse."

"Oh, here you go," Rayna says, smiling cheerfully. She holds up a sweatshirt, along with a tote bag that I'm sure I didn't bring with me.

I snatch my items from her and shove Tate out the door, anxious to get started with whatever he has planned. Anything to get out of there. Shrugging into my jacket, I hope it's long enough to cover the wet mess that must be all over the back of my sweater and pants. Just once, I'd like to spend time with Tate without having to wash my clothes.

Chapter 18

Joy

"So, are you going to tell me where you're taking me?"

Tate flashes a smile before returning his attention to the road. "I can tell you if you really want to know. I already gave you pretty big hints."

I scoff. The only thing I was able to get out of him as we headed to my house so I could change, was that I should wear jeans and boots. That's pretty much all I wear anyway, so I wouldn't call that a hint. I'm torn between the suspense killing me and wanting to be surprised. I'm still undecided when he pulls into the entrance of a fast-food place.

"Okay, I'll give you a hint." His smile would make my knees weak if I wasn't already seated. "It's nearly two hours away, so I figured we might want to eat first."

I laugh. None of his hints have been actual hints at all. It's only been a few days since I've seen him, but I've missed him. The crinkles around his eyes deepen as he continues to smile at me. It does things to me. I'm not sure if it's how sexy his smile is, or how rare it is, but it literally takes my breath away.

"Fine, just surprise me. I'll have the nuggets and fries combo."

We make small talk while we eat, and it isn't long before I've forgotten how badly I want to know where we're going. There's something about riding down country roads on a sunny day. It's early spring, so flowers are just beginning to bloom, and green buds are sprouting on the trees.

Tate places his hand on my thigh and gives it a squeeze as he pulls onto a gravel driveway. As the trees clear, I can see a huge plot of land in front of us. It's all fenced off, and there are horses scattered about. And then I see the stable. It's a huge structure, with red distressed wood making it look like a painting and not real life.

"Where are we?" I'm in awe as I take in my surroundings.

"This place made me who I am."

Tate doesn't say anything else as he pulls into a gravel parking area and finds a spot. I know there's a story behind it. From what I understand, Boulder Ranch has been hosting the rodeo practically forever. And Boulder Ranch is next door, while this place is hours away. Accepting Tate's offered hand, I step out of the truck and fall into step beside him.

"My dad's best friend owns this place," he explains. "When I was little, we came down here nearly every weekend. They host the rodeo, so even though we didn't necessarily come down for the rodeo, I watched everyone practice. I was obsessed. Riding broncs is where I started. But once I was old enough to get on a bull, it was all over. I was hooked. And then I started going to Boulder Ranch."

I swallow hard. "And you just wanted to show me?"

Flashing that panty-melting smile, he shrugs. "Yeah. I was thinking about you while I was here, and I realized how much you'd probably like the equestrian center."

"The building we passed when we first came in?" I ask excitedly.

He smiles and nods. "Yeah. I remember what you said about your aunt so..."

"Holy shit, that place is huge!" I squeal. "It's okay that we're here? Can we go inside?"

"Of course. I mentioned to the Eglestons that I would like to show you this place some time, and they insisted. And when I suggested today, they also insisted we stay for dinner."

I'm practically vibrating with excitement. This place is much larger than Boulder Ranch. The arena and stands seem to be similarly sized, but the rest of the ranch makes Boulder Ranch look like some small private property. The equestrian center is probably twice as big as the stables I help take care of. Tate points out different buildings as we walk to the equestrian center, but I'm not paying attention. My focus is on the beautiful land.

Once we reach the building, Tate takes my hand before opening the door and leading me inside. I'm at a loss for words. For as large as I thought the structure was from the outside, it's probably twice that size. There are barrels set up and I stop to watch a girl with two long braids lead her horse around them. The woman standing at the entrance with a stopwatch cheers when she passes.

We walk further into the building and nearly every stall is occupied. I thought Boulder Ranch housed a lot of horses. There's no stopping the grin that spreads across my face as I look around the facility. When we get to the far end, Tate spins me to face him, and I'm momentarily lost in his disarming gaze.

"What do you think?" he asks.

I do a slow spin and look around one more time before I answer him. "I think it's amazing. I've never seen anything like it. Thanks for bringing me here."

Tate leans forward and brushes his lips against mine in a tease of a kiss. He moves to step back, but I grip his shirt and pull him close, capturing his mouth with mine. He briefly smiles against me before taking control and sliding his tongue against mine, finally ending with a gentle nip.

Our silence is comfortable as we slowly move to the other end of the facility, stopping to visit each horse along the way. I can't get over how clean the place is. All of the stalls seem freshly cleaned and it doesn't smell unpleasant. I briefly wonder how many people help run this place. We come to a stop to watch the girl practice. Aside from the roughstock events, barrel racing has always been my favorite. I wish I hadn't let my mom talk me out of learning. One of the trainers at my aunt's facility had a background in it, but I passed up on the opportunity.

"You okay?" Tate's voice startles me a bit, completely derailing my train of thought.

"Yeah. I was just watching her. I've always loved barrel racing."

"You know how to ride. You should give it a shot."

I stare at him, wide-eyed. "I don't know how to ride like *that,*" I protest. "And I am thirty-three years old. Way too old to be falling off a horse trying to do something cool."

Tate chuckles and pulls me close before returning his attention to the arena. I'm not sure how long we watch the young woman practice, but I could have probably watched all night had a sweet voice not interrupted us.

"Tate, honey, I'm so glad you made it back here."

I turn to find a woman who appears to be in her late fifties approaching. She's pretty, and not the sweet grandma-looking type. Her skin is tanned, and she's wearing an off-the-shoulder tee, boot-cut jeans, and worn cowboy boots. Her brown hair is streaked with gray and piled on top of her head in the perfect messy bun. She's very pretty in an effortless kind of way. If it wasn't for the smile lines and slight crow's feet around her eyes, I would mistake her for my age.

"Hi, Mrs. Egleston. Thanks for having us," Tate says, pulling the woman into a hug.

"Tate, don't go calling me that just because your beautiful friend is with you." She turns and directs her attention to me. "Hi, honey, I'm Martha. I've heard a lot about you. It's nice to put a face with the name."

I reach out my hand, but she pulls me into a brief hug. "Thanks for having us. This place is amazing."

"Oh, sweetheart, you're welcome anytime. You both are. If you're interested, you two can ride a few trails before supper. John will likely be out working for another hour or so."

My ears perk up at the suggestion of a trail ride. I've been dying to get back to it ever since my first time at Tate's. There's nothing better than enjoying nature while on the back of a majestic animal.

"Really? Can we?" I look from Martha to Tate, and back.

"Yeah, come on," he says before turning to Martha. "We'll be back in time for supper."

Martha is an amazing cook. I didn't even realize how hungry I was until I started eating. But each bite was so delicious, I just couldn't stop. I sip my coffee and look around the table, watching the conversation I'm not paying attention to. This feels a lot like some version of meeting the parents, and I don't hate it. John is just as friendly and welcoming as Martha. He doesn't look as young as Martha, but judging by his strength and energy, his age doesn't mean anything.

"Can I get you another piece of pie?" Martha offers.

"Oh, I couldn't, but thank you. I'm not even sure how I managed to eat so much. Everything was delicious," I respond.

"Oh, thank you; I'm glad you enjoyed it. Will you be staying the night? I wasn't sure, but I went ahead and got a room ready." Martha stops clearing dishes while she waits for a response.

My brows shoot up. Tate never said anything about staying the night anywhere. Well, Tate really didn't say much of anything at all. It's a bit awkward since we haven't even been seeing each other for long, but I don't hate the idea.

"What do you think, sweetheart?" Tate asks while he places a hand over mine. "If you want to leave, we can. If you want to stay, that's also okay."

Tate keeps his voice low, and Martha has gone back to clearing the table and chatting with her husband. The conversation is just between the two of us. I'm not sure how I should answer, so I shrug.

"Joy? It's okay if you want to go back. This is like a second home to me, and it's practically a bed and breakfast as often as they have people staying here. Wherever they put us it will be somewhere private. But I'm also fine driving home. It's your call."

My call? "Well, what do you want to do?"

He looks down before a shy smile slips free. "I kind of like the idea of stealing you for a little getaway."

And just like that, I don't care what we do or where we go, as long as he looks at me like that. Shy smile still in place, his dark eyes search mine. His gaze is intense, but I don't want it to leave me. I feel like he's seeing all of me, and I like it.

"I don't have clothes..."

"Yes, you do. In the bag Rayna packed for you," he says, interrupting me.

"Wait. What?"

"We'd love to stay," Tate says, speaking loud enough for John and Martha to hear. "Is it my usual room?"

Martha nods as she loads the dishwasher. "Yes. Same room. There are two sets of towels in the bathroom and an extra blanket on the bed. Holler if you need anything."

I follow Tate to the room. It's early, but all I want to do is take a shower and put on clean pajamas. My smile returns as I think about the fact that Tate planned this whole thing. Tate thought of me. It probably shouldn't be that big of a deal, but it is to me. It's all I think about as I wash off the smell of outside and horses. It's all I think about as I crawl into the bed and into his arms. It's all I think about as he slides a hand over my naked body, teasing along until he reaches my already wet center.

Chapter 19

Tate

As soon as I step out onto the porch and lay eyes on the stables, I breathe a sigh of relief. It was hard to concentrate on the meeting, knowing Joy was so close but I couldn't see her. Smile, nod, sign, and repeat. There's still time before the lineup, so I head directly to where I know I'll find her. I haven't laid eyes on her since I stole her away for the night.

I find Joy in the tack room putting things away, and I watch her for a few minutes without her noticing me. She's quietly swaying and dancing as she works. Eventually, I clear my throat, but she can't hear me over the music in her ears. When she finally turns and sees me, she jumps in surprise.

"I'm sorry," I say, raising my hands while I wait for her to remove her earbuds. "I tried to get your attention, but you didn't hear me. I didn't want to grab you..."

Smiling, she closes the distance between us and presses her soft lips to mine. "Sorry. I shouldn't have had my music that loud. I just didn't anticipate anyone coming to find me in here."

"I missed you. I couldn't wait another second to look at you." I kiss her forehead. "I'm sorry my schedule has been so busy since we got back."

"I thought I saw your truck when I pulled in."

"You probably did. I've been here all afternoon, but I was in a meeting," I explain.

I wait for her to ask more about why I was here, but she doesn't. "You're going to be late."

I grin at her and place a kiss on her lips, lingering longer than I planned. "You trying to get rid of me, darlin'?"

She takes in a sharp breath and looks up at me through her thick lashes. "No. I—um—just don't want you to be late. And I want to get this finished, so I don't miss your ride."

She's right. I am going to be late. The meeting took longer than I'd expected, but there was no way this wouldn't be my first stop. I want to tell her all about it, but I can't. Not yet. But my nerves are settled just from laying eyes on her.

"I'll meet you by the gate after my ride." I brush a kiss along her temple. "Will you be there?"

With a smile and a nod, she returns her attention to what she was doing before I interrupted. As much as I hate walking away, I need to get ready before the opening ceremony. I tune everything out as I make my way to the locker room, passing by cowboys who are doing all they can to stay focused. I remember all too well how hard it was to ignore distractions when I was first starting out. Keeping to myself, I head over to my locker and get ready. I'm still securing my chaps when it's time to line up.

"Please stand and remove your hats for the singing of our National Anthem," the announcer says over the loudspeaker.

As soon as that song is over, we return are hats to our heads and take our places around the rolled up American flag, in time for the beginning chords of Courtesy of the Red, White and Blue. Adrenaline pumps through my veins the same way it always does during every opening ceremony. We've unrolled the flag in time to the music and pyrotechnics, the crowd cheering along as we do. It's hard not to get wrapped up in the pomp and circumstance of the ceremony. My gaze collides with Joy's as I hold my end of the flag.

"...God bless the USA and God bless our troops." There is a moment of silence before the announcer continues. "Last month we told you about some changes coming to the Cole County Rodeo. Tonight, we are pleased to announce the new ownership. Tate Garrison will be taking over Bolder Ranch. As a long-time bronc rider and bull rider here in Cole County, we are confident that there couldn't be a better set of hands to keep up with the legacy."

I zone out as they continue the introductions. There is no easy way to announce an organizational change as significant as this. Even though this place has been a huge part of my life for as long as I can remember, this is still a major change. My gaze doesn't leave the section of fence where I agreed to meet up with Joy. Even though she knew the ranch was coming under new ownership, she had no way of knowing it would be me. All I can do is hope she'll hear me out.

I go through the motions, smiling and posing for a picture here and there. It's all white noise in the background as I prepare for my first ride. Die-hard fans fill any available open seats, and before long, I'm left alone with my thoughts as I get my head straight. Things are much easier when there's no time to consider the questions or the consequences. Questions and consequences I never had to worry about when I was alone. I never really worried if Gray would get pissed about anything; he's always pissed at me anyway. He never got over me leaving for the rodeo circuit without him. But now I can't stop thinking about Joy and what she's thinking right now. Even as I get ready to face my brother.

I try my best to shake off my argument with Gray as I make my way into the saddle. Of course he wouldn't fucking hear me out after that announcement. All I know is, I need to talk to him again before he rides. I don't care if he stays pissed at me, but his head needs to be on his bull. On autopilot alone, I take control of the bucking bronco I've been assigned. He's not interested in me riding him, but it's as if I can anticipate every one of his movements. I move my feet and rock my body like it's the only thing I'm capable of doing. My feet move in time with his movements, and it doesn't feel like long before I hear the buzz of the time clock. Eight seconds are over.

The cheering from the crowd is my only clue that I've somehow managed to do the right things. Glancing at the gate, I quickly search for the only person I want to see cheering for me. But her spot is still empty. I take my hat off and wave at the crowd before briefly dropping to one knee in thanks, then rush out of the arena before they've announced my score. The only thing I'm worried about is finding my girl.

"Joy?" I call her name as I enter the barn. "Joy, are you in here?"

"Do you need something?"

Turning toward her voice, I find her sitting on a bench against the wall. She doesn't smile at me or move to stand. She also doesn't look very busy.

"Is everything okay?" I ask cautiously.

"Is everything okay?" she echoes. "Is everything okay? I don't know, will I get fired if I answer honestly?"

All I can do is stare at her in confusion. It's clear she's pissed, but she lost me with that statement.

"You didn't tell me. You didn't think I should know I was getting ready to have sex with my *boss*?"

My stomach drops. I didn't even think of it like that. There's no way I should have pursued her knowing she works at the ranch. When it comes to her, I seem to forget about a lot of things. The expression on her face reminds me why I've been happily avoiding relationships before now. Because the look on her face is causing the most painful ache in my chest, and I'm not sure I'll be able to fix it.

"I swear I didn't think about it like that. No one knew I was buying this place. I wasn't specifically keeping you out of it. I was told not to talk about it until they made the announcement."

"Yeah. But that doesn't change the facts. I'm not sure I can do this."

I stand momentarily frozen, her words landing like the strike of a hand. "What are you saying? Just because it changes things doesn't mean they've changed for the worse."

I don't want to leave this barn until we get things figured out, but I hear them introduce Gray, and I didn't get to see him again before his ride. Another reminder of how much easier things were when I was alone. I allowed myself to get distracted, and I'm already letting things fall to the wayside.

"I just need some time to think. It was already complicated enough just with you being tied to the ranch as a bronc rider. But now you're my boss. It's a lot to take in," she says with a sigh of defeat.

"Okay. But promise me we can talk about this. It doesn't have to be now. Tomorrow?"

"I work at the doctor's office tomorrow. And then I have to come in here for a few hours."

I glance toward the arena to try and see if I have time. It looks like he's about ready. "Okay, I'll bring you lunch, and we can talk. I'll be at our spot watching Gray and the rest of the bull riders if you change your mind and want to talk to me tonight. Or stand with me."

I make it outside just as the gate swings open from the chute and Gray's bull comes flying out with a purpose. Making my way to the gate, I stop when I hear my name. To my surprise, Joy is rushing after me. I thought, if anything, it would take her some time before she was ready to face me. She smiles hesitantly, but my attention is dragged away by the collective gasp from the crowd.

I turn to see my brother in a heap on the dirt, a bull fighter hovering over him protectively. The bull must have run after him once he'd been thrown off. But that's not what's concerning. What's concerning is that the bull has been corralled, and my brother still isn't moving. The crowd is silent as I hold my breath and wait. Joy's arms snake around me in a comforting embrace, and just as I'm about to gently push her away so I can get to Grayson, I see him begin to stir.

Chapter 20

Joy

"Can I get you anything, Mrs. Garrison?"

It takes me a moment to realize the nurse is speaking to me. "Oh, no, thank you. I'm okay. I'll probably go on a coffee run soon anyway."

We've been at the hospital most of the night. When Gray didn't get up after getting thrown off the bull, all hell broke loose. Tate refused to leave his brother's side; I refused to leave Tate's side. River stepped up and has been holding us all together, taking charge and making sure Gray received the proper care. Well, until we got to the hospital and this asshole doctor showed up. Now, I'm afraid to leave Tate's side because I can tell he's about to lose his shit.

"You can go for coffee," Tate says softly. "I'm fine."

He's not fine. I doubt he even believes himself. I was hoping Tate would be less on edge once Gray returned to his room, but he's still leaning forward in his chair with his elbows resting on his thighs as he stares at his brother. My heart feels like it's been torn in two. One half goes to Tate and the other to River who is still in the waiting room. The only reason I've been allowed back is because Tate told the nurses that I'm his wife. When we told them that River is Gray's wife, the nurse just gave a sad smile. Dr. Buckner had already made sure to tell the entire staff that River was not immediate family and not on his case.

"I'll stay here with you until he wakes up. Or until they let River back here."

A low, humorless laugh rumbles out of him. "You don't have to babysit me. If I haven't beat the shit out of that asshole doctor yet, I'm probably not going to."

"That's not—" I start to argue, but his stern gaze causes my lie to falter. "I just want to make sure you're okay."

I swallow hard as I look at him. He looks broken. Dark circles surround his eyes and his jaw is set. His lips form a grim line, and they barely twitch as I correct my lie. I do just want him to be okay. And part of being okay is not getting arrested for assault.

"Thank you," he breathes before returning his gaze to the hospital bed.

I wish I knew what to say. Or what to do. The last thing I said to Tate before shit hit the fan was that I needed space to figure out if I could do this. I still need space, but I'm not leaving him here alone. Not like this. I place my hand on his back, preparing to rub it, but he instantly sits up and then leans his body toward me. Opening my arms in invitation, I wrap them around him when he leans his shoulder against mine and rests his head back against the wall. No, I definitely can't leave him like this.

I must have fallen asleep, because next thing I know, Tate is kissing my forehead and giving my shoulder a gentle shake. The curtains are drawn, so it's hard to tell how long I've been asleep or what time of day it is. Gray still appears to be sleeping.

"What's wrong?"

Tate smiles and shakes his head. "Nothing is wrong. They are going to let River come back if you want to go on that coffee run. Or if you want to go home and get some sleep..."

"Oh," I said, breathing a sigh of relief. "That's good. How's he doing? Did I miss anything while I was asleep?"

He kisses my cheek before sitting back in his seat. "He's doing okay. Squeezed my hand when I told him we were still here."

I feel every muscle in my body noticeably relax as more relief rushes through me. That has to be good news. I feel okay about leaving to clear my head. And I can't miss my shift at the ranch. Especially not now. At least I know he won't be alone. He'll have River here with him.

"That's so good. Better than okay." I place my hand on his thigh and give it a squeeze. "What do you want for breakfast? I have time to grab something before I head to the ranch."

Tate is quiet as he studies me. His eyes are serious, but he gives nothing away even as he hesitates to respond. "I'm not really hungry, but I'll eat whatever you want to bring me. Thank you."

I squeeze his hand before I stand to leave because I still have no idea how to not be awkward. Fortunately, he doesn't seem to notice with all his attention on his brother. Meanwhile, I'm silently dying. I feel like I'm supposed to be with Tate. Even after telling him it wasn't going to work if he's my boss, I didn't think twice about driving him to the hospital or sitting with him while we all wait for Grayson to wake up. Even now, I hate the thought of leaving him. I've already decided that after my shift at the ranch, I'm going to shower, change, and come right back here.

Chapter 21

Tate

Relief hits me like a tidal wave. After focusing on the sound of River's retreating steps, I finally allow myself to take my first deep breath since seeing Gray on the ground. My lungs expand with much-needed air, and I finish with a cough when my breath catches. He's awake. And he's talking. I held my breath for what felt like the entire time he spoke to River before she left to give us some time. He's still tired, but he's finally making purposeful responses. He's okay.

"Jesus Christ, Gray," I rasp before closing my eyes and starting again. "I'm glad you're okay."

He holds my gaze for a long moment before he blinks and looks away. I watch as I can only assume the moments leading up to his trip to the hospital replay in his mind. His expression goes from groggy, to angry, and finally shaken up before he forces it back to neutral. He's always trying to prove something. He should be shaken up. *I'm* shaken up and I didn't even see it happen.

"Yeah, it would be a real waste to buy the Millers out and not have a chance to rub it in my face."

For a moment I'm glad he's in a hospital bed recovering from a terrible injury. It's the only thing keeping me from laying his ass out. He loves to paint me as the bad guy. And I prove him right every goddamn time.

"Grayson, not every fucking thing is about you. Do you really think I live my life just to find ways to piss you off? Gary came to me, and I couldn't say no. The ranch is one of the few things life hasn't ruined for us. I couldn't risk someone else buying it with no interest in keeping it going," I say, before finally uttering the words I should have years ago. "You're all I've got, Gray. I'm not trying to be an asshole all the time; I just want what's best for you."

His eyes remain focused on mine before he swallows hard and looks away. His slow nod tells me he heard what I said, but the conversation is over. The last thing I want to do is leave things like this, but in the hospital moments after he woke up from a head injury probably isn't the best time to push. He's always pissed at me, anyway. It can wait till he's out of here.

"We can talk about it later. Anyway, I'll send River back in here. I'll check back."

Standing, I pat his shoulder before walking out. It doesn't help that all this happened the one time I didn't get back to see him before his ride. All I could think was that he had to wake up so I could tell him I bought Boulder Ranch for *us*.

I don't get far before I run into Joy. Her arms are full, with a tray of coffee in one hand and paper bags in the other. Looks to be the same items as yesterday. She looks beautiful, not like a woman who spent the night in an uncomfortable hospital chair only to go directly to work at the crack of dawn and then repeat the cycle all over again the following day. She only left last night because I demanded she go get some rest. It was only fair after she insisted I take her car to go home for a nap and a shower while she sat with Grayson.

"Hey. Let me help carry something."

She angles the coffee toward me and I take it before we step to the side. "Sorry, I'm late this morning. I couldn't find parking at the cafe, then I forgot my purse and had to go back to my car."

"Hey," I say in a low voice, stepping closer. "Don't apologize. You did something nice for me. I wasn't timing you. Thank you."

She takes a slow breath and then nods. "You're welcome. Were you on your way out?"

"River is in there with him. I figured I'd give her some time since we were in there for an entire night before they even let her back. But I can wait if you want to see him. He's awake."

Her face lights up. It's the first smile I've seen since I stopped by the barn before the opening ceremony that changed everything for us. Before she found out I was the person taking over the ranch. "Oh, that's so good! I'll just see him real quick when I bring River her breakfast. I'll be right back."

She rushes off toward Grayson's room, and I rake a hand through my hair as I try to figure out what to say to her now that we know he's going to be okay. Now that we can finally breathe. It's awkward, and that's my fault. I should have told her about the ranch. Not that it would change anything, but she didn't deserve to be surprised right along with everyone else. So, I tell her as soon as she returns to my side.

"I'm sorry I didn't tell you. I should have."

She looks up at me, surprise written all over her face. "Yeah. You should have."

Before I can say anything in response, she turns and starts walking. I follow her through the lobby and out the main entrance to the sidewalk where she stops. "My place or yours?"

I clear my throat in surprise. "I'm sorry, what?"

She tilts her head. "Your truck isn't here and after being up most of the night worrying about you and Gray, I'm only driving one place. So, your place or mine?"

That's right. She drove. I guess I would have figured it out once I reached the parking lot. She does look tired. Gorgeous, but tired. There's a slightly purple hue below her eyes and her lips are curved into a frown. I'm feeling about the same way.

"My place, since my truck is right there."

"I don't care how close it is—" she starts before I cut her off with a glare.

"I wasn't suggesting you drive home after taking me to my truck. I was just saying it would make getting my truck easier. I'd rather not be alone right now, anyway. I know you said you need to figure things out, and that's fine. I just need... someone."

Her eyes widen a fraction as she looks at me. Really looks at me. It doesn't take long before her shoulders relax just enough for me to notice. Then she nods her head.

"Yeah. Yeah, okay. You don't have to be alone," she says with a forced smile.

I can't tell if she's trying to convince me or herself that she's doing the right thing, but I'm too tired to try to analyze anything. Relief has given way to exhaustion, and all I want to do is get in my bed and close my eyes. She must realize I'm tired down to my bones because she doesn't say anything else. Simply gives me a sad smile and leads the way to her car. When I lean my head back and close my eyes the second I get into her passenger seat, she places a comforting hand on my thigh but still says nothing as she pulls out of the parking lot in the direction of my house.

Chapter 22

Tate

I wake with a start. It's dark and it takes me a moment to realize I'm in my bed. I was in such a dead sleep that I don't even remember my head hitting the pillow. A brief panic hits me when I remember why it's been so long since I've seen my bed. Just as quickly as it hits me, the panic begins to fade. He's okay. He's awake and still just as pissed at me now as he was after the announcement.

I prop the pillows behind me and lean against the headboard, scrubbing a hand over my face as the fog of sleep slowly begins to clear. When my eyes adjust to the dark, I see a figure curled up beside me. Joy. One leg hangs out while the rest of her is wrapped up in the throw blanket I usually keep at the end of the bed. One *bare* leg hangs out. She isn't wearing pants. It doesn't matter that I can't see in the dark, that doesn't stop me from instantly recalling what those legs felt like wrapped around me.

Squinting at the clock on my bedside table, I find I haven't actually slept all day and night even though it feels like it. It's 9:00 at night. Growling in my stomach reminds me I haven't eaten anything since the breakfast sandwich and coffee Joy picked up from the café across from the hospital. I still can't believe she drove back and forth, forgoing sleep, just to be there for me and to make sure River and I ate. Definitely above and beyond considering we've been in limbo since just before Gray got hurt.

Trying my best not to wake Joy, I carefully slide out of bed to make my way to the bathroom. She doesn't stir, so I leave the door cracked and do what I have to do using nothing but the glow from the nightlight. She must be exhausted. I half expected to wake up to an empty house.

My stomach growls again, letting me know that I need to eat if I plan to go back to sleep. With my eyes adjusted to the dark, I see Joy has stretched out a bit more, revealing more of her naked thigh and the book she must have been curled up with. I'm not sure when she went to sleep, so I decide not to wake her before I head to the kitchen in search of food.

There are no leftovers since I haven't been home to cook. Needing more than a quick snack, I scan the fridge for something fast and easy to make. My eyes land on a package of cheese. Grilled cheese sandwiches. Perfect. I grab the butter and sliced cheese, set them on the counter beside the bread, and get started.

"Hey."

My back stiffens at the sound of Joy's voice behind me. I finish flipping the sandwiches over before I turn around. And it's a good thing, because goddamn. My eyes trail over her still half-naked figure, and it's several long seconds before I remember how to speak. Instead of one of my T-shirts, she's wearing a thin white camisole with the outline of her nipples visible in the dim light of the kitchen, and a pair of simple pink panties. *Holy fuck.*

"Did I wake you?" I finally ask as I turn around to press down on the sandwiches with a spatula.

As I wait for her response, I silently beg my dick to behave. I'm a thirty-eight-year-old man, I should be able to control myself. I turn back around to face her once I remove the grilled cheese sandwiches from the stove and place them onto a plate. Her eyes travel the length of me and I'm painfully aware that we are both standing in the kitchen half dressed. I'm not even half dressed, standing here in just my boxer briefs.

"No," she breathes. "You didn't wake me. I guess I'm just awake for the same reason you are."

"Hungry?"

Her gaze drops down for a split second before returning to my eyes. Smirking, I grab a second plate, placing two of the four sandwiches onto it before passing it to her. Disappointment briefly crosses her gaze but vanishes as she looks down at her plate.

"I don't want to take your food," she objects.

"Sweetheart, I am not going to eat four grilled cheese sandwiches."

Leading the way, I walk to the small kitchen table and pull out a chair for Joy before taking the opposite seat. She has a confused look on her face as she picks up a sandwich and takes a bite. Then, she closes her eyes and moans. She fucking moans, and I have to shift in my seat to adjust my hardening cock.

"This is delicious. You cooked for me even though I was sleeping?"

I meet her eyes, and once again I forget my words. She's always beautiful, but sitting across from me, her hair a mass of thick, unruly curls, no makeup, and no walls up, I can't look away. I've never had anything like this before—someone who shares my space and immediately makes it better just by being here. I clear my throat to try and get rid of the tightness in my chest.

"Of course, I made enough for you."

"Thank you." She gives me a small smile before starting on her second sandwich.

Grilled cheese is one of my specialties, so it doesn't take long before I'm paying attention to my food and not the look of surprise on her face just because I made her something to eat. When I glance back up, she lets out a small chuckle and presses her teeth into her bottom lip.

I raise an eyebrow and swallow the last of my sandwich. "What is it?"

"I was just thinking about the first time I was here."

Memories of that night instantly flood my mind. I remember every second I've spent with her, so it doesn't take much for the vivid images to begin replaying. The way she looked wearing my clothes. The kiss in the rain. Our shared midnight snack. Lounging under the blanket, watching that insane documentary. The expression on her face when she came apart around my fingers. The way she melted at my words of praise.

When I return my attention to her face, her eyes are on me. "And the last time I was here."

I lose the battle over my now fully erect dick. It took an inordinate amount of strength to get out of bed with her lying there. But I haven't forgotten her words to me just before Gray's accident. She ended things. Said she can't do it. She asked for space.

"Joy, we should talk."

"It's late. It's been a long few days. I don't want to talk."

My brain screams at me to shut this down. I do my best to avoid messy situations, and I already know she's it for me. If we do this and then she decides she doesn't want anything more with me, I'm not sure I'll recover from it. But after these last few days, there's nothing I'd rather do than lose myself in her.

"Please."

The raspy word from her lips is enough to lure me to my own destruction. I don't give a fuck what happens to me after this. The first night she was here, I turned her down. I wanted her even more than I wanted my next breath, but I sent her away because I thought she deserved someone who could give her more. The look on her face still haunts me. Combine that with how fucking bad I need to feel her body beneath mine and there's no way I'm going to tell her no.

"Sweetheart, is this what you really want? I won't be the one to stop this; I'm not that good of a man."

She stands and rests her hand on the back of the chair. "All I care about is right now. And after the past few days, we need this."

Goddammit. I told her I wouldn't be the one to stop this, but I can't help my hesitation. She didn't answer my question. Didn't say she was sure this was what she wanted. But she's right. I need to lose myself in her, even if it's just a short break from reality. If she decides she doesn't want to be together just because I own the ranch, I'll figure that out.

She doesn't move from where she stands beside her chair. Her peaked nipples strain against the thin fabric of her top and her breathing quickens under my gaze. Without any further hesitation, I stand and am in her space after just a couple long strides.

"I should put a stop to this," I say before covering her lips with mine.

As soon as our mouths connect, heat courses through me and I pull her close, so our bodies are flush. Her soft frame melts into mine as I slide my tongue into her mouth. There's no turning back. I've missed her mouth. And her touch. The stress of the last few days melts away and is replaced by desperate need.

Chapter 23

Joy

Tate's rough hands graze my heated flesh as he slowly drags my thin shirt up my body and over my head. His gentle touch doesn't match the hunger in his eyes. He's gentle but commanding as he continues backing me further into his room.

There was never any question that I would stay with Tate while we anxiously waited for Gray to wake up. In just a few short weeks, these people feel like family. Gray and River are more than just people I see in passing. Being there for Tate while trying to keep some distance between us has been absolute hell.

"Joy," he rasps, his words warm against my neck. "If you want me to stop, just tell me, and I will."

"I know."

My thighs hit the mattress, causing me to gasp in surprise. Tate pulls away and his eyes search my face as he frames it with both hands. I don't move. I barely breathe as I get lost in the intensity of his gaze. He finally steps forward and covers my mouth in a kiss that takes the last of my breath away. It's slow. And sensual. It's all consuming as he holds me still, and works his mouth against mine, teasing and tasting with his tongue.

Moaning, I wrap my arms around him and pull him closer. All of my tension, and worry, and anger have turned into desire so strong I'm worried it will consume me. Reaching a hand between us, I stroke his hard length through the thin layer that separates us.

"Fuck, sweetheart," he hisses, pulling away just enough to briefly rest his forehead against mine.

I keep still when he slowly slides his hands down to my neck, to my shoulders, and finally down my arms where he takes both my hands in his. My heart constricts. I was expecting fast and dirty. A way to get it out of our systems and relieve the stress of the past few days. Not this. I close my eyes and swallow hard, trying to get control of my emotions.

"You're perfect," he whispers.

Still holding my hands, he slowly lowers to his knees and presses a kiss to each of my palms before releasing them. The sight of him on his knees before me is nearly too much to handle. His eyes remain on mine as he slides his hands up my thighs and rests them on my hips.

"I'm sorry for not telling you."

"No." I cut him off before he can continue. "Please. I don't want to think about it. Right now, it's only us."

His eyes hold mine and he hesitates for a fleeting moment before sliding his fingers into the waistband of my panties and sliding them down. The way he's looking at me… It's raw. Vulnerable. I close my eyes and bury my fingers in his hair, using him to keep my balance as I step out of my panties. His muttered curse sends a jolt to my already throbbing core.

"Tate," I whine. "Please."

Sliding his hands back up my thighs, he grips my right leg and drapes it over his shoulder, leaving me completely exposed. *Holy shit.* The heat in his eyes has my core clenching. I'm certain he can see how wet I am, and it only heightens my desire.

"Tate," I whimper.

Without a word, he holds my gaze as he brings his mouth to the apex of my thighs. He swipes his tongue across my sensitive slit and my knees nearly buckle. My mouth pops open in a silent scream when he spreads me wider and spears his tongue into my entrance. I can't think. I can't move. I can barely remain upright as I feel myself already spiraling toward release.

His beard is rough against my sensitive skin which adds to the sensations as he circles his tongue around my clit. My chest constricts and I let out a noise I don't even recognize when he clamps his mouth around me and sucks, drawing my clit into his mouth. He slides one hand up and grips my ass, steadying me when my knees buckle.

"Fuck! Tate!"

My breathing comes in short gasps as my orgasm builds. His hair is soft on my fingers as I grip it and tug, which only seems to make him greedy for more. He slides his hand from my thigh to my center, slipping two fingers into my pussy and sending me crashing over the edge. Screaming a garbled version of his name, I struggle to remain upright through the most powerful orgasm I've ever experienced. Static fills my vision as I continue to pulse and squeeze around his fingers.

"Look at you, soaking my face. So, fucking good."

"God—" I can't manage another word when his fingers are stroking that sensitive place inside me, drawing out my pleasure.

"Say *my* name when I'm making you come," he growls.

"Tate!"

My legs give out, and he stands with ease and lowers me to the bed. Did I just—I don't have a chance to finish my thought before he strips off his only piece of clothing and joins me on the bed. He hovers over me, looking me over briefly before crushing his lips to mine, plunging his tongue into my mouth.

"See how good you taste?"

He returns his mouth to mine before I have a chance to answer. I haven't fully come down from my orgasm yet, but I already want more. Heat builds in my core from the sweet tang of my arousal on his tongue. He kisses me like I'm his lifeline.

I wrap my arms around him and pull him closer, raising my hips in a desperate plea for him to fill me. He teases at my entrance and I'm ready to beg. I need him. Finally, he slides a hand down to my waist and holds me steady as he slowly glides inside. My breath catches at the unfamiliar sensation of skin on skin, the feeling alone causing need to coil tighter at my core.

"More," I cry as I meet his thrust, trying to take him deeper.

"Fuck, sweetheart, I—fuck—I should get a condom."

"I'm on birth control."

His only movement is his breathing as he studies me. "Are you sure?"

"Yes. I want to feel you."

I know this could be our last time together, and I want there to be no holding back. I want all of him. He draws back and then fills me again, deeper than the last time. Stretching around his hard length, my pussy squeezes him as he sets a steady pace. I run my hands along the corded muscles of his back, holding him close and enjoying the way they move and flex beneath my hands. His hair, now damp with sweat, hangs in his face as he looks down at me.

"Fuck, Joy. Your tight pussy is the perfect fit for me."

His words. God, his words. And the way he's looking at me. He grips my thigh, just above the knee, and raises it, spreading me wider as he pistons into me. His thrusts grow harder, and I meet each one. I crave the delicious line of pleasure and pain that I'm teetering on. My body trembles, and before I know what's happening another orgasm tears through me. Dragging my nails down his back, I bite down on his shoulder as I come apart on his cock.

Tate kisses my forehead and down my cheek, until he reaches my mouth. The kiss on my lips is soft. Tender. I swallow the lump in my throat as he places more soft kisses along my jaw, stopping just below my ear.

"On your knees. Ass up."

Chapter 24

Tate

Joy is fucking perfect. Gripping her hip with one hand, I trail my other hand up her naked back, once again working hard to maintain control. It took everything in me to not come apart with her, and I'm close again just from this view of her amazing ass.

I line myself up at her entrance. She jolts at the contact, and I use my free hand to caress her back until she relaxes. As soon as she does, I slide myself into her, groaning at the way her pussy grips me. She's already beginning to tremble.

"Tate," she whines. "It's too much."

"You can take it."

I pull out before slowly thrusting back into her, and she lets out a low moan. She meets my next thrust and cries out. Her sounds are all it takes for my control to snap. Gripping her hips, I slam her to me. I repeat the motion again and again, setting a steady pace. Every nerve in my body tingles as I feel my release getting close.

"You're beautiful," I breathe. "So, fucking perfect."

"Tate!" she cries out. "Oh, shit."

Leaning forward, I speak softly against her ear. "Yeah, baby? You ready to come for me?"

"I—I can't," she pants. "It's too much, I can't!"

"Yeah, you can," I say gently, snaking my arm around her to tease her clit. "You can give me one more."

Her cries grow louder, and her body stiffens around me. "Tate—I—I—"

"*Fuck,* Joy," I growl as my balls tighten and my breathing grows even more shallow. "Fuck!"

I feel her squeeze around me as her entire body stiffens. My orgasm crashes through me and I swear I might black out. Her pussy continues to clamp around my pulsing cock as I fill her. She collapses and I follow, turning us both so I don't land on top of her. We're silent as we lay still trying to catch our breath.

She's quiet when I drag myself out of the bed and head for the bathroom. Leaving the door open, I quickly get cleaned up and prepare a warm washcloth for her. She's still quiet as I join her on the bed and gently wipe away our mess. After tossing the washcloth into the hamper, I finally get back in bed, covering us both with the blanket.

"You okay?" I rasp, placing a kiss on her bare shoulder after pulling her into my arms.

Her back is pressed to my front, so I can't see her face, but I feel her tense in my arms at the question. My heart picks up speed as I force myself to give her a second to respond.

"Did I hurt you?"

"I'm okay," she says after another long moment.

"Did I hurt you?" I repeat.

She shakes her head. "No. I'm okay."

I'm not believing that for a second. Once again, I force myself to give her time to talk. Her arm is silky and warm beneath my touch as I stroke her in a soothing gesture. Another long silence stretches between us and it's obvious she isn't planning to elaborate.

"Sweetheart, listen—"

She cuts me off. "I meant what I said. I don't want to talk tonight."

Her tone is final. Hope begins to fade as I recall the ways I fucked up. I can beg her forgiveness all I want, but when it comes down to it, I'd be fucking pissed too if things were the other way around. But she's here. She gave her body over to me in a way I've never experienced. She allowed herself to be vulnerable with me, even after I hurt her. And she's still here. That means something. It has to.

I want to argue. To push for her to talk to me, but I know nothing good could possibly come from it. So, I pull her a bit closer and enjoy the fact that she's here and allowing me to hold her. I brush her hair from her face and place a kiss on her cheek before returning my head to the pillow. Her comforting scent fills my nose, and when I feel her breaths growing slower and more even, I close my eyes.

Chapter 25

Tate

It's been five days. Five fucking days since I woke up to find Joy gone from my bed; and she's avoiding me like the plague. As busy as I've been with the transition at Boulder Ranch, I still can't think of anything but her. I hate my empty house. I hate walking past her car in the parking lot and not being able to storm into the barn and demand she talk to me. Well, I guess I could, but that would only prove her point about this being a problem.

"Well, boss, what do you think so far?" Hayden's gaze lingers on me for a moment before returning to the arena where a few of the guys are getting in some practice rides.

"I haven't really done much yet, but running this place while I have my own working ranch is going to be a problem. I knew it when I agreed, but now I really need to find someone. I'd rather have someone help me out here than hire more staff for my place," I say with a sigh.

I can't complain about how much work it is because I know what I signed up for. What I don't say is that my first thought when Gary first approached me, was that maybe Grayson would help me run it. Now, I'm not sure. He'll be okay, but between his recovery and his new relationship, it might be asking too much.

"While you get it figured out, you know I'm good to help you out at your ranch here and there when you need it."

"Thanks." I pat him on the back once before returning my attention to the arena.

It feels strange watching the guys practice without participating. I only have a few minutes until my next meeting. Gary was so adamant about keeping everything a secret that we didn't start meeting with current business associates until after the papers were signed. That means there is a lot to do in a little bit of time. The Millers can stay in the house as long as they want as far as I'm concerned, so they've been gracious enough to work with me and help me along with the transition.

"How's Gray doing?" he asks after a few of the practice rides have been completed.

"He's doing really well considering. He's home. Was told if he takes it easy and completes his follow-up appointments, he'll be back to normal before he knows it."

"Good," Hayden says without taking his eyes off the next rider.

Hayden is a good man. He takes care of those he's close to. He's one of the few people I'll ask for help when I need it. Since he's lived on a ranch his entire life, I know he can take care of it without me having to explain in great detail how each thing should be done. And I've gone to help him in a pinch as well.

Even though we don't typically get along and things have been—well—strained since what feels like forever, Grayson is one of the only other people I would extend that kind of trust. He might not think twice about trying to beat the shit out of me, but he'd never take it out on my animals or an innocent bystander. We may seem like enemies, but brothers are forever.

As I stand at the gate enjoying the last few minutes of freedom I have before my next meeting, I feel someone's eyes on me. The hairs on my neck stand up as I scan the barn. Finally, in the far corner, I see a familiar figure with her arms crossed. I can't make out her expression and she turns away as soon as my eyes begin to focus. After only a couple steps toward the barn, I change my mind and turn back. I can't chase her here. I let out a deep sigh of resignation.

"Alright, Hayden. I'll see you around."

I have a few minutes before my meeting, but I know if I stand here in view of the barn and stables for much longer, I'll end up storming in there to demand Joy speak to me. This pull I've always felt between us only seems to grow stronger the longer she avoids me.

Before I reach the steps leading to the office portion of the main house, Gary steps out onto the porch. His long, silver hair brushes across his shoulders when he folds his arms and looks at me.

"Already wishing you were out there with them instead of stuck going to meetings with me all day?" He pauses to laugh. "Well, it's too late, you already bought the place. This is your life now."

I look from Gary's ripped jeans to the missing sleeves of his T-shirt and realize I probably don't need to walk around this place in Polo shirts and my nice jeans every day. Gary and Rhonda have always been down-to-earth, so it's a safe assumption that they do business with similar types of people. So far, every meeting we've gone to has been relaxed and informal. It's a lot of work, for sure, but since I already own a ranch, most of this isn't new.

"It's not that bad," I say with a short laugh. "At least I still see the people I've been spending my summers with all these years."

Gary nods in agreement. "It's hard work, but it doesn't feel like it when you're having a good time. Especially when you're young. We're getting tired, and the look on Rhonda's face when I told her I was ready to retire and move to the Southwest makes it all worth it. And we can do that since we know this place is in good hands."

Pride swells in my chest, and I look at the older man across from me for a long moment before I speak. "That means a lot. Thanks. I'll take care of this place."

"I know. Anyway, Rhonda sent me after you. She wants us to have some lunch before the next meeting."

I raise an eyebrow. Rhonda is always trying to feed me and make sure I don't need coffee or iced tea or whatever it is she has on hand. But the next meeting is set to start in about five minutes. It's just a conference call, but still. I can't exactly hold a conversation with a mouth full of food.

"Do we have time for that?" I ask.

"Yeah." He gives me a nod before leading the way inside. "The call got moved back thirty minutes. I sent you a text."

I didn't even check my phone while I was outside taking a breather. I watched a few practice rides and chatted with a few people. I pull it out with hope that maybe I missed a text from Joy as well, but there's only the message from Gary. Joy takes up all my free thoughts. I would take her yelling at me over avoiding me. She has a few more days to avoid me before I end the silent feud. I'm not going to send her a bunch of texts or call her phone nonstop. But I will talk to her here if I have to.

CHAPTER 26

JOY

I can't believe I am this fucking drunk on a Tuesday. It's River's fault. Now that Grayson is doing much better, River is back to being pissed at him because, of course, he doesn't want to listen to her and take it easy. And since I've been avoiding Tate, I didn't have any reason not to go out for a drink when she offered. As I struggle to focus on the words across my phone screen, I'm kind of wishing I had said no.

"Rayna or Wyatt will come get us. I'm seventy percent sure I texted her and asked her to," I slur. "Don't look at me like that, this is your fault."

We both burst into a fit of giggles before I restart the same conversation we've had at least thirty times tonight. "I just can't believe Tate didn't tell me. I can't fuck my boss."

"Sure, you can. You already did. But what am I going to do about Gray and his stupid, stubborn ass? I mean, I get why he's pissed. If anything, he has more reason to be angry than you do. You haven't been seeing Tate for long. Tate is Gray's brother. He should have told him. But *still.*"

"He should have told us both. And now he wants to talk, like it's not too late." I roll my eyes as I finish the last of my drink.

The past two weeks have been a blur. I don't even remember what I wanted to say to Tate when I chased after him. I keep thinking about what he said. Just because things have changed, it doesn't mean they have changed for the worse. We got involved before I had any idea he was buying the place. And I believed him when he told me he didn't think about it from that angle. That's why I've been avoiding him. I know if he talks to me and brings reason and logic to the situation, I won't be able to resist. I'm not sure I *want* to resist, and that's what's so damn scary. I can't trust my own judgment after I spent all those years in a relationship oblivious to the fact that it was headed nowhere.

"Darlin', you didn't have to go through all this trouble just to see me."

The hairs rise on the back of my neck as the familiar voice washes over me. The voice I've been avoiding since we knew for certain Gray was going to be okay. Slowly, to avoid making the room spin, I turn around and lock eyes with Tate. He looks good. Too good. He's wearing a pair of well-loved jeans and a blue and gray flannel shirt. His hair is damp as it hangs beneath his hat, and I have to fight to keep from running my fingers through his curls.

"What are you doing here?" My question comes out more weary than angry.

"Taking you home."

I shake my head but don't put up a fight when he tosses several bills onto the bar and carefully grabs my arm to help me from the stool. I gasp from his touch as I feel it travel all the way through me. His simple touch is the thing I've missed most by avoiding him. I didn't realize until right now just how much I needed it.

"How did you even know I was here?"

"Rayna called me. She said you texted her something unintelligible and asked if I knew where you might have gone with River. This was my first stop."

"Well," I say with a huff. "I'm fine, and I'm not leaving River alone. So, you can go now."

I have to look away from his lopsided grin. And when I do, it's just in time to see Grayson walking over. River gives me a wide-eyed look before returning her attention to the younger cowboy as he joins us.

"Let's get you home," Tate says in a low rasp.

My resolve is gone, so I accept his hand and follow him out the door. I don't object when he reaches over me and buckles my seatbelt. I even lean into him when he presses a kiss to my forehead. Closing my eyes, I soak in his scent as it surrounds me and allow my mind to wander as he pulls out of the parking lot. When not enough time has passed before he places the truck back in park, I give him a quizzical look.

"I said I was taking you home," he says simply. "And don't look at me like that. You're drunk and we need to talk before anything else happens between us."

I blink in surprise, trying my best to ignore the way his words travel straight to my core. The way he showed up looking like a freshly showered knight in shining armor, and then the sweet forehead kiss, have my thoughts completely scattered. I want him. And I've missed him. But he's right; we do need to talk first.

"Fine," I acquiesce. "But don't take the couch. I don't like being alone in your bed."

Swallowing hard, he nods in agreement before speaking in a raw voice. "I didn't bring you here so we could both be alone."

I watch as he steps out of his truck and quickly rounds the front to open my door. I figured he would have been done with me by now. I haven't talked to him since I slipped out of his bed while he was still sleeping. I ignored his calls and didn't answer his texts. When I set out to get trashed with River, this is the last place I expected to end up.

He opens the door, and when I accept his hand before stepping out, I feel the same jolt I felt the first time we touched.

The walk inside is short and quiet. He says nothing as he leads the way to his bedroom. Silence stretches over us as he begins stripping off his clothes. I allow my gaze to drag over his bare chest before I finally follow and begin removing mine.

He tosses me a shirt from his drawer before he climbs into bed and waits. His bed smells familiar, and I feel better the second the soft sheets touch my skin. I don't hesitate to crawl into his open arms, laying my cheek against his chest.

Tate lets out a low groan and presses a kiss to the top of my head. "I'm glad you drunk texted Rayna."

Lifting my head from his chest, I look at him. "Why? Looks like you were either headed to bed or on your way out. Either way, plans ruined."

He lets out a low laugh. "Neither. I had just showered after evening chores. I wasn't headed to bed just yet."

I glance at the clock. It's late. Very late. "At this hour?"

"Yeah. Running two ranches makes for a long day."

I study his face. His eyes look tired, and his beard isn't as neat as it usually is. He still looks good enough to take my breath away, but it looks like the long hours are taking their toll. Reaching up, I stroke his cheek, savoring the feel of his beard against my palm.

"You look tired. Are you going to hire help since you have two places to run?"

He takes a slow breath and absently runs a hand over my hair, running his fingers through the strands when he gets to the ends. "Yeah, I have Hayden giving me a hand here, and I'll get Boulder Ranch figured out soon. But I'll be fine for now."

"Tate, you're exhausted."

He heaves an annoyed sigh. "Yeah. I know. I'm exhausted because I've barely slept since you left that morning."

I swallow hard as I'm hit by a wave of guilt. I shouldn't have left that way, and I shouldn't have ignored him afterward. But I couldn't see a way to make it work, and I wasn't ready to say goodbye. I'm still not sure it can work but being in his arms like this gives me hope.

"Tate..."

"We'll talk tomorrow." He places another kiss on the top of my head. "Right now, I just want to get some sleep now that I finally have you in my arms."

Chapter 27

Joy

Time's up. There's nothing left to do but talk. We had coffee and ate something light before going out for morning chores. I feel much better than I thought I would. In fact, I feel pretty good. Tate looked shocked when I joined him in the kitchen wearing one of his sweatshirts and the jeans I had on last night. Even if I was hung over, I would have suffered through, knowing how buried in work he is.

"Toast?" Tate has two slices of bread in the toaster and holds up the loaf as he waits for my answer.

"Sure. Thanks."

He places bread into the two empty slots. "You ready to tell me why you left here the way you did?"

I let out a small gasp in surprise. I knew it was talk time, but damn. I was hoping we would ease into it. Taking a sip of my coffee, I watch him over the rim as I try to explain the crippling anxiety I felt at the thought of facing him. It wasn't our first time together, but I've never felt so raw. So stripped bare and exposed. Yet none of that changes the fact that he's my boss. Or that he kept it from me.

"I was afraid to face you," I admit in a low whisper.

"Have I done something to make you afraid to talk to me? What were you afraid to say? You're safe to tell me anything you want," he promises.

I take another sip of the hot coffee and try again to think of some words. "I'm sure you don't think it's a big deal, but you lied to me. You lied by omitting something so important. I struggled enough with you being associated with the ranch I work for."

Tate removes the toast and places it on a plate with the bacon and sausage, and I follow him to the table with the plate of eggs and potatoes. His gaze lingers on mine as he takes the seat across from me, but he doesn't say anything. He simply gestures for me to fix my plate.

"I'm sorry. I really am. If I could go back in time, I would tell you on the first night. But we talked about this already. And then I thought you changed your mind. You came after me. You stayed with me at the hospital. You took care of me..."

His voice cracks on the last word and that's all it takes for my walls to come crashing down. Suddenly, none of it matters. Boulder Ranch doesn't matter. What people think doesn't matter. I'm not the only one who's been stripped bare. His elbows are on the table as he rests his chin on his clasped hands and watches me closely.

"Of course I stayed with you..."

"Why?" His hoarse voice is barely above a whisper.

"I tried to walk away. I tried to leave you alone." My eyes burn with unshed tears as I try to find some words to fix this.

His eyes linger on mine before he averts his gaze and turns his attention to his breakfast. I'm not hungry. My stomach is in knots, but I force myself to take a few bites. The food is delicious, but I barely taste it as I worry about what's next for us. Everything I said holds true, but I'm not sure I'm ready to let him go.

"If you don't want to do this—if you really want this to be over..." He drags a hand over his beard and swallows hard before he continues. "If this is really over, I'll take you home. I won't hunt you down at work. I'll leave you alone. But this isn't corporate America. Ranches and farms like this are family-owned and run. You're a good worker and everyone knows it. Decide for yourself, not because you're worried about what people might think."

Warm tears escape and I try to wipe them away, but it's pointless. I don't want it to be over. I tried to convince myself I did. All the time I spent avoiding him, I tried to forget him. I tried to forget the way he makes me feel. I tried to forget how safe I feel in his arms.

"I don't want it to be over," I admit. "I just don't know how..."

He's out of his chair and crouching beside me before I even get the words out. He looks up at me and places his hand on my shoulder, slowly sliding it up to cup my jaw. Closing my eyes, I lean into the comfort of his touch. Avoiding him has been absolute torture.

"You don't have to know how. We'll figure it out together," he says gently before placing a kiss right beside my lips. "If you want, I'll pretend like I don't even know you when I see you at the ranch. And I promise to make sure to fire you if you start slacking."

Somehow, I find myself laughing. "Well since you put it that way..."

Laughing, he stands and pulls me from my chair and into his arms. I breathe in his scent, allowing it to calm me. I barely reach his shoulder, making it easy to get lost in his hugs. This is what I needed. No matter what lies I told myself, there will be no walking away from this man. If things between us end, we'll both leave with bruises and claw marks. It's terrifying. And comforting.

He places another kiss on the other side of my mouth before finally pressing his lips to mine. This kiss is slow and gentle. Tentative. Keeping one hand on my lower back, he slides the other one up the back of my neck, holding me in place as he deepens the kiss. Finally, I begin to relax. We still have a lot to figure out, but at least I know we'll figure it out together.

Chapter 28

Tate

Shifting my truck into park, I look up at the newly constructed ranch-style house in front of me. I've been here before, but not like this. Not to try to have a conversation with my brother that I really need to end with a handshake and not a fight. His truck is in the driveway, but since he's still technically not supposed to be driving, that doesn't really mean much.

With a heavy sigh, I place my hat on my head and step out of the truck. I don't make it all the way up to the porch before the door swings open and Gray appears.

"Was wondering if you planned to get out of your truck or just sit there all day," Gray says with a smirk.

"How you feeling?" I ask as I climb the last two steps to the porch.

He shrugs before stepping outside and gesturing for me to have a seat. "I'm fine. Did you come all the way out here to ask how I'm feeling?"

I let out a wry laugh. This shouldn't be so hard, but I guess it's my fault. Looking back on the past several years, it's not hard to understand why he thinks I do nothing but give him shit all the time. It doesn't matter that I didn't mean to come off that way. I did. And I didn't try to change. All I can do now is talk to him and hope I'm not too late.

"You still pissed at me for Boulder Ranch?" I ask.

Gray studies me for a long moment before he responds. "I'm not pissed. I just think it's bullshit that I can't have one fucking thing for myself. It's not enough that you also compete there once a month like I do?"

"Gray, listen," I begin, stretching my arms out. "I'm not even going to compete like that anymore. If it was about winning, I wouldn't have bought the place. I bought it for *us*."

He stares at me in confusion, hostility all over his face. "What the hell do you mean, you bought it for us?"

"I bought it because I couldn't stand the thought of someone else buying it and then getting rid of the rodeo and bull riding after we practically grew up there. I bought it and hoped you'd be interested in helping me. Something that could just be for us."

He continues to stare at me. "What?"

"Gray, listen. I'm so sorry for how things have been, but I really hope we can get past it. We haven't always been like this.

I think we can work together or something. If you want. Just let me know."

"Work together?" He looks at me, confusion etched in his features.

"Yeah. As in, help me run the place. You don't have to give me an answer right now, but I really need the help, so the sooner the better. I'd rather have you there then have to hire a stranger I can't trust." I stand and reach out my hand. "Promise you'll at least think about it?"

He zeroes in on my hand for a moment before he finally reaches out and takes it. "I'll let you know."

Relief floods through me with those four words. Hell, the fact that we got through the conversation without a screaming match or any punches thrown feels like a huge win. This conversation was a long time coming. I still feel like shit for the way things have been between us. As the older brother, I should have handled it better. But hopefully, this is the start of a new beginning for us. Only time will tell.

Thoughts of fresh starts flash across my mind as I make my way to the truck. I honestly couldn't have imagined a better way for our conversation to go. I need help at the ranch. That's a fact. And it is the honest truth that I would rather have that help come from my brother who I trust despite not always getting along.

"Tate. Hi," Rayna greets me as soon as I walk into the Family Health Center. "Joy is with a patient. She didn't tell me you were coming, or I could have done the intake for her."

"Don't worry about it. She didn't know I was coming," I respond, holding up a paper bag from the market. "Did you all eat? I stopped and picked up some sandwiches."

Rayna's smile stretches as she looks from me to the bag, and back toward the exam rooms. I promised to be discreet when we're at the ranch, but this isn't the ranch. Rayna is Joy's best friend, Dr. Robinson already knows, and the nurse doesn't work on the days Joy works.

"You came out this way just to bring Joy lunch?" Her smile grows wider.

"I brought you lunch, too." I reach into the bag and pull out a sandwich wrapped in butcher paper. "Smoked turkey melt."

Her eyes widen, and she leans forward to reach for her sandwich. I didn't want to show up with food as if Joy was the only person here. But I would be lying if I didn't also do it for selfish reasons. I'm hoping Rayna won't give me shit since I thought of her.

Rayna returns her attention to me just as I hear the exam room door open. Joy walks out with her face still buried in the tablet so I use the opportunity to drag my eyes over her. This isn't the first time I've seen her in scrubs, but each time I lay eyes on her I find something else to appreciate. The black scrubs are loose but cling in all the right places to remind me what's underneath. Her curls are pulled back in a ponytail showing off the delicate curve of her neck.

"Oh. Hi," she says with a gasp when she finally looks up.

"Hey." I step closer and she stiffens before glancing at her friend. "I brought lunch."

She relaxes a bit at the sight of the bag. "Oh. Thanks."

I knew she might get upset at me showing up at her work, but I didn't think it would be this awkward. I want to pull her to me. I want to kiss her and tell her how much I missed her. But something tells me that's not the way to go.

"Did you eat, Tate? Joy, I can cover for you if you want to have lunch together," Rayna offers.

I shake my head in answer to her question to me, and Joy offers a flat smile. "Thanks."

I follow her down the hallway and out the back door to a small patio where we sit at one of the picnic tables. I'm quiet as I pass out our food. Hopefully she explains why she's acting like a stranger, so I don't have to come out and ask.

"I'm sorry," she begins after a long silence. "I just wasn't expecting to see you here. Thanks for bringing lunch."

"I didn't think it would be a problem since Rayna is your best friend and knows about us."

Her hand covers mine. "No, it's not a problem. I was just surprised. And it still feels weird being around people, knowing I work for you."

I should have been expecting her to respond this way, but I was really hoping things would be back to normal since it's been a few days. Even with our awkward exchange, being around her calms me after the interaction with my brother.

"You okay?" she asks.

When I look back up, she seems back to her old self. Her shoulders are relaxed, and she has a small smile as she meets my gaze. This is what I needed. Somehow in this short period of time, she has become the thing I need when something is missing. She grounds me.

"Yeah, I'm better now. I just left Gray's place and wanted to lay eyes on you."

Her smile widens and she finally picks up her sandwich and takes a bite. She's adorable, closing her eyes and nodding to herself as she enjoys her first taste. I could watch her all day.

"Is he okay?"

"Oh, yeah he's fine," I reassure her. "I went over to see if he'd be interested in helping me run Boulder Ranch."

She straightens in her seat. "Oh? Did it not go well?"

I let out a snort. "I guess it could have gone worse. He didn't throw me off his porch or anything."

"He said no?" Her voice is quiet.

"Not exactly. But he sure as hell didn't say yes. He looked at me like I'd finally lost it. Like he couldn't even comprehend the idea of working together. The whole reason I agreed to take the place over was because of the stupid hope that we could run it together."

Explaining it aloud makes me feel even worse. Of course he'd think I've gone crazy. The only person who knows my feelings is me because god forbid, I talk about them. I would if I ever knew what to say. The only way my brother will know that I'm the way I am because I care, is if I tell him. So, I'd better figure it out.

"He didn't say no. If he was that against it, he would have shut it down right away. Don't give up."

"Yeah," I agree. "You're right. I'll figure things out in the meantime. I knew I came here for a reason."

She gives me another smile before returning to her food. I feel a million times lighter after sitting here and talking for just a few minutes. I'll give Gray time to think about it and get back to me. And I'll see just how much Hayden is willing to help until I find out for sure if I need to hire someone permanently.

"Thanks again for surprising me with lunch," Joy says, standing to collect our trash.

"Thanks for—well—being you. Come over tonight?"

"I don't know..." she says slowly as she tosses our garbage into the nearby trash can.

Walking up behind her, I place my hands on her hips and pull her close. I breathe in her scent before pressing a soft kiss to the top of her head. "Do you have some reason not to?"

"I guess not," she says quietly.

"Good. I'll see you at 6:00."

"That's dinner time," she points out.

"Exactly. I like to see you with your mouth full."

She lets out a gasp and swats me playfully. "Tate, I'm at work. You can't say things like that."

I let out a low chuckle and then kiss her temple. "I'll see you tonight where I can say whatever I want."

I turn and walk out. There's no need for me to turn and look; I can feel Joy's gaze on me as I push the door open and walk outside to the front parking lot.

Chapter 29

Joy

I'm a fraud. Tate Garrison as my boss was nearly a deal-breaker for me. I'm independent. I don't want any preferential treatment or for anyone to think I have this job because I'm sleeping with the boss. Well, if that's true, I need to figure out why one glimpse of him has my heart racing and my thighs clenching.

He's been extra careful to keep things at the ranch strictly professional, but when he walks past looking the way he looks, I'm the one struggling to pretend like I don't get to see him naked. Especially when I catch other women like Miranda paying close attention to him. I want to shout that he's mine, keep your eyes to yourself.

"It's going to be so weird tomorrow with neither of the Garrison brothers riding." I look up to find Miranda standing beside me. Speak of the devil.

"Oh. Hey, Miranda." I'm less than excited to see her.

"Hey. Is Tate nervous?" she asks.

I feel bad keeping her at a distance when she's truly only ever been kind to me. But I still don't feel completely comfortable with people knowing about my relationship with him. Shifting my stance, I prop a foot up on the gate.

"I'm sure he's fine. He knows how to run a ranch, and he's helped out behind the scenes at the rodeo even before," I respond carefully.

"You realize you don't have to pretend, right?"

Doing my best to hide my surprise, I turn to face Miranda. She looks at me from her spot along the gate. Her hazel gaze narrows in on me as she waits for me to respond.

"What are you talking about?" I ask when she doesn't elaborate.

"Girl. Be for real. I knew you and Tate were a thing when you rode in together after that rainstorm, no matter what you said. Ever since then, he looks at you like no one else exists. It's cute."

Gaping at her, I try to find a response without looking like a fish out of water. "What do you mean?"

Tipping her head back, she laughs. "I mean we all know. If it isn't busy here tomorrow night, just go 'head and be there with him. This isn't the big city. Literally, nobody cares."

I open my mouth and then shut it without saying anything. It's a bit of a relief that I don't have to keep things a secret anymore. Honestly, it was less about the job than it was about what people thought of me. I thought it was bad wondering if people would see me as a buckle bunny, but sleeping with the boss felt huge. Even if my job isn't the start of some prestigious career, I really expected people would care. I desperately want to believe Miranda.

"Think about it," she urges. "Anyway, are you going to the Thirsty Pony? I'm sure you know a bunch of us are going as a kickoff to Tate's new rodeo career."

"Yeah, I'll be there."

"See you later, then." With a smile and a wave, she turns and heads back into the stable.

I'm finished for the day, so I head to the gravel parking lot and to my car. I'll have just enough time to shower, get some housework done, and then get ready. I was worried about keeping up appearances, but if Miranda's telling the truth, maybe it isn't such a bad idea to join everyone at the Thirsty Pony.

"Hey, you heading out?"

Looking up, I meet River's gaze as she laughs at what I can only assume is a look of shock on my face. I'd been completely lost in my head and didn't even see her in front of me. I laugh along with her before answering.

"Yeah. Will I see you tonight? At the Pony?" I ask.

She shrugs. "I'm not sure. I'll go if Gray goes."

"Is he coming to watch tomorrow? I'm sure Tate would love it. It would even be a good excuse to see if he's interested in helping out."

Now it's River's turn to look lost. With eyes narrowed, she repeats what I said. "Helping out?"

"Tate's drowning in work. He gets up and does morning chores before coming here. And then he's out late on his ranch after his day here is over."

River looks more confused with each passing second. "And he asked Gray?"

I let out a short laugh. "Yeah. He bought the place with the hope that Gray would want to work with him. He stopped by his house to talk to him a little while ago. Guess he didn't tell you."

River is quiet for a minute before she crosses her arms. "I'll see if I can get him to come out tonight. He didn't talk to me about any of that, but maybe he'll be motivated to either talk about it or make a decision if they're in the same room together."

"Good luck. Maybe I'll see you later," I say with a chuckle before continuing to the parking lot.

All I can do is laugh and roll my eyes. I knew the men were stubborn and I knew they didn't get along from day one. I signed up for this. It may sound like a terrible idea, but the best thing these Garrison men can do is be forced to spend some time together.

Chapter 30

Tate

"You ready for tomorrow?"

I've answered the question for what feels like a hundred times in the fifteen minutes that I've been here, but I smile at Miranda as I give her a confident nod. "If I can ride bulls and broncos that do their best to throw me off, I can be the man behind the scenes."

Miranda laughs and pats my shoulder before walking away. On the inside, I can't wait to go home. But, I keep a smile on my face and do my best to appreciate all these people being here to celebrate with and support me. Doing my best to respect Joy's wishes, I suggested she meet me here instead of showing up together. I've been scanning the room for her since I walked through the door.

Hayden takes the bar stool beside me and gently elbows me in the ribs. "Just know, when I go out there and win tomorrow night, I would have even if you were competing."

Laughing, I flag down the bartender and order us both a round of drinks. Having a drink with Hayden is a hell of a lot better than feeling like I'm on display. Ordinarily, I would turn down something like this. I'm no one important. Boulder Ranch has been a part of my life since what feels like forever, so it's not crazy that I would take over to make sure the Cole County Rodeo doesn't disappear. Every season we see new talent. Every year another kid with more heart and ambition than sense spends his summers here learning how to stay on a bull. And if I can get enough help running the place, I plan to offer more programs for the local kids to learn about this lifestyle.

Feeling someone touch my back, I turn to find Joy standing behind me. Her smile causes me to momentarily forget how to speak, so I just smile back at her like an awkward teenager who doesn't know how to talk to girls.

"Hey," she says, leaning forward to kiss my cheek.

She kissed me. In public. This time it's confusion stealing my ability to speak. This woman was so against anyone knowing we're together. Now, here she is, kissing me in public. It's just a kiss on the cheek, but still.

"Hi?" My greeting comes out more like a question, causing her to laugh.

"Dance with me?"

I feel Hayden's eyes on me as I turn completely around on my stool to face Joy. Her smile grows and she steps close enough to casually trail her fingers along my thigh. That tiny bit of contact has my heart speeding up. I ignore Hayden's laugh as I down my drink and stand, taking Joy's hand in mine.

"You're looking at me like you've seen a ghost," she says once I have her in my arms on the dance floor.

The music switches to a faster song, but I know the steps, so I pull her to me, helping her to follow along. "Last we talked about it, you were set on keeping things quiet."

Stepping back, I hold up our joined hands so she can spin before pulling her close again. Her smile is radiant, and her eyes gleam when she looks up at me. "Yeah, I changed my mind."

"Oh yeah?"

"Mm hmm," she hums. "I never used to hide. I don't want to start now. Plus, apparently everyone already knows about us. And you were right. No one cares."

The laugh I'm trying to hold in escapes as a low rumble. It doesn't matter why she changed her mind. I'm just glad I don't have to pretend like I'm not aching to touch her every time I see her. I'm a grown man, so of course I don't plan to put on a show, but I don't want to pretend like we're just friendly acquaintances. And I don't want to pretend to be single.

Having her in my arms this way reminds me of the day we met. Our connection was impossible to ignore. Even when she was yelling at me. Seeing her again at the bar, and getting my hands on her? That only solidified things.

"I won't say I told you so."

Laughing to herself, she allows me to pull her close as the music slows. Her scent invades my nose, so I close my eyes and breathe her in. I really need Gray to come through with the help, because I don't get to spend time with my girl nearly as often as I'd like. Most of the times are when she insists on coming over to help around my place.

"I was already tired of working so hard to not look at you. And then when Miranda asked about you, she pretty much laughed at me when I tried to answer as just a person who knows you. She told me everyone already knows, and like you said, no one cares. But I still don't want us to be like this when I'm at work."

"Of course. I'm just glad I get to do things like this." Barely swaying to the music, I lower my lips to hers.

She welcomes my kiss, parting her lips and swiping her tongue along mine. We made up weeks ago, but this is the first time I'm not weighed down by the heaviness that started the night she said she couldn't do this. It finally feels like we might make it through, after all.

"Even if people do have a problem with us, I'm not sure I care anymore. I was miserable without you. And yeah, I was pissed, but Grayson's accident taught me that there are more important things to worry about."

I kiss her again, this time it's less chaste, and I have to remind myself that we're in the middle of a crowded bar. Her body molds to mine as we continue swaying. I'm not sure how many songs go by as I continue to hold her and appreciate the warmth of her body against mine.

Eventually, the music switches over to a popular line dance, but I'm not ready to let go of her. "You want to get out of here?"

With an eyebrow raised, she looks up at me. "These people are here for you. Do you really want to skip out on your own party?"

"With you? Hell yeah, I do." I laugh. "This isn't a party. We just all agreed to meet here for some drinks. I'm here. I had drinks and talked to everyone I wanted to talk to. Right now, I just want to get you home. Naked. And in my bed."

Her breath catches and I watch as her pupils dilate. She nods her head and gives a breathy affirmation that does nothing to discourage my hardening dick. Hayden catches my eye and smirks. I give him a nod but otherwise ignore him as I fight to keep from dragging Joy from the bar. As soon as we reach the door, I pull it open and nearly collide with Wyatt and Rayna.

"Are you guys leaving already?" Rayna asks, looking around me to pin her gaze on Joy.

"Yeah." Joy makes a big deal out of yawning. "It's been a busy day. I'm really... sleepy."

Rayna cackles and looks from me to Joy several times before she shakes her head. "Uh-huh. Tired. You two better go get some—rest."

"Oh, we plan on it," I say. "Lots of rest."

Joy elbows me in the ribs but doesn't stop laughing, even when I grab her hand and pull her out the door. I should be able to control myself, but with her, I don't want to. We practically jog to my truck, and I can't stop myself from pulling her in for one more kiss before I round the front of the truck and to my spot in the driver's seat. She tastes so damn good.

Chapter 31

Joy

My skin is heated, my breaths come in short gasps, and my body is coiled tight when my eyes flutter open. It takes me no time to figure out why. Tate's tongue makes slow, leisurely swipes up and down my center. Sleep still lingers in the background as my body spirals toward release.

"Tate," I breathe, curling my fingers into his hair.

His expression when he looks up to meet my gaze is nearly enough to send me over the edge. Slipping a finger inside me, he sucks on my clit and it's enough to toss me completely over with a guttural cry as my muscles tighten. I release around his finger, waves of pleasure washing over me.

"Morning, darlin'. Fuck, you taste good."

Catching my breath, I keep still as Tate kisses his way up my body until his eyes are level with mine when he smiles down at me. Eyes I could get lost in. I'm not sure how I managed to avoid him for as long as I did. Or what made me think I would be able to stay away. I've never had a man make me feel this way, and even with all the reasons I should stay away, it's just not possible.

I part my lips to respond, but he covers them with a kiss, sliding his tongue into my mouth. Tasting myself on him causes a new spark of heat to spread through me. I'm still a bit sore from last night, but when he lines up at my entrance, I eagerly accept every inch as he slides into me.

"Holy—" I lose my words when he drives into me with a claiming thrust.

Chuckling, he buries his face in my neck, gently licking and sucking as he sets a steady pace. I'm barely awake, yet another orgasm is already barreling down on me. But it's not enough. My hips meet every thrust, and my hands greedily caress the planes of his back.

"More," I breathe. "Tate, I need more."

Without breaking our connection, he shifts, gripping my hips and changing the angle so he can take me deeper. Goosebumps spread across my naked flesh, and I cry out when he hits that spot that's so deep, and so sensitive, all I can do is hold on as waves of pleasure roll over me.

"Fuck, Joy. That's right, baby. Let go for me."

And I do. I surrender to the sensations, chanting his name as I feel him follow with his own release. He rolls off me and immediately pulls me to his chest, holding me close as we both come back down to earth. I breathe him in, enjoying his earthy scent.

"Good morning to you, too," I say with a laugh once I'm finally able to speak. "It's not even light out."

Tilting his head, he presses a kiss to the top of my head. "I have to get started on chores but couldn't go out there without tasting you."

I shouldn't have this reaction to his words after two orgasms that were so strong I nearly blacked out. "If you wanted me to help, you could have just asked."

"No, sweetheart. You stay here and relax. I'm serious. Hayden will be here to help out today, so I won't be long. Go back to sleep."

I open my mouth to argue, but he presses a finger to my lips before replacing it with his mouth. The kiss quickly turns from chaste to heated, and I could almost cry from the loss when he pulls away. His expression is stern, leaving no room for argument.

"Fine," I say with a resigned sigh.

Turning to my side, I watch in silence as he pulls on a pair of jeans. As much as I enjoy him naked, there's something undeniably sexy about watching him get dressed to go out and do work on his ranch. His fingers deftly secure his belt after his T-shirt is pulled on along with a flannel button-down. As much as I want to help, it feels good to lie in bed for a bit. I'm not a morning person, so usually by the time I'm awake, I'm already running late.

With a kiss to my forehead, he leaves the bedroom and gets started with his day. As good as the bed feels, there's no way I can go back to sleep. I give him a few minutes before making my way out of the bedroom and to the kitchen. He doesn't need my help with farm chores? No problem.

"What's all this?"

I turn away from the stove to find Tate watching from the doorway of the kitchen, his arms folded as he leans against the frame. My eyes make their way up and down his body, from the worn jeans that fit him just right to the rolled-up sleeves revealing his muscular forearms. I could never grow tired of looking at this man.

"I figured you'd be hungry once you finished out there, so I made breakfast." I gesture to the breakfast bake sitting on the stove beside a plate piled high with bacon and sausage before glancing down at my bare legs. "I made plenty in case Hayden was still with you. But I thought you'd be a little longer."

Slowly, his lips curve into a grin. "You cooked me breakfast?"

My smile matches his as I make my way over to him for a quick kiss. "You told me not to help with chores, you said nothing about cooking breakfast."

"No one's ever cooked me breakfast before. And no. You think I'd bring him in here when I left you naked in my bed?"

Swallowing hard, I fight the unexpected sting of tears when he gently brushes my cheek with the back of his fingers. The gesture is so gentle. Filled with reverence. It makes me sad to think he's never had anyone do something as simple as cook him breakfast. I can't say I'm surprised, since he seems to have spent all his time trying to care for everyone and everything else. Including Boulder Ranch.

Before I can come up with a response, he captures my lips in a kiss before pulling back to study my face once again. "Thank you."

Walking into the kitchen, he heads for the sink, leaving me staring after him as he washes his hands and then takes two plates and two mugs from the cabinet. It's like we do this every morning. I join him at the counter and pour coffee while he fixes his plate.

"You have a long day ahead of you. I just wanted it to start off right," I say with a nervous shrug.

"I love you."

Judging by the look on his face, his words took us both by surprise. Warmth spreads through my chest as his words sink in. I don't have to think about it. I love him too. Once again, I find myself blinking back tears as I part my lips to respond.

"You don't have to say anything," he breathes. "I just needed to tell you."

I must look like a deer caught in the headlights, but it isn't because I don't feel the same way. It's because I do, and it's fucking terrifying. I thought I loved my ex, and maybe I did. But it was nothing like this. Trying to stay away from Tate, no matter how noble I thought my reasons, was torture because I couldn't continue to ignore my feelings.

"I love you too."

Chapter 32

Tate

What the fuck was I thinking, taking this place over without having any help, or a plan? I'm beyond exhausted. So exhausted that I blurted out the three words I never thought I'd say to a woman. Not even twenty-four hours after she finally decided to stop giving a shit about what people think of our relationship. I continue to pace inside the barn, trying to get my head right.

"Tate?" Joy's voice interrupts my spiraling. "Are you okay?"

I look up to meet her gaze. It's no wonder she came looking for me. I insisted she come back here instead of going straight to Boulder Ranch tonight, but I've been avoiding her since she got here.

"I'm sorry. Just came out to clear my head," I admit.

"How can I help?"

Surprised to hear that response, all I can do is stare at her for a moment. After inviting her here only to ignore her, she's asking how she can help instead of telling me that I'm being a dick. If Gray ever decides to talk to me again, I'll have to thank him for making me lose my temper that day. If I hadn't been leaving the doctor's office when I was, there's a good chance I would still be miserable and alone. Albeit I didn't realize how miserable I was until I allowed happiness to seep into my life.

"Sweetheart, you're already helping. Come here."

Tilting her head, she eyes me for a moment before straightening and closing the distance between us. She looks so good, if I was just riding, I'd suggest we skip tonight. She has on a pair of tight jeans that show off her soft curves and a tight black T-shirt paired with her trusty boots. Fucking gorgeous. I hold out my arms and she steps right inside, squeezing me in a desperately needed hug. Instantly my nerves begin to fade as I relish in her touch. I've gone my entire life without this. Without someone who makes me feel like things might be okay. Someone to make me believe maybe there is a reason I'm here.

"You ready?" My chin brushes the top of her head when I speak.

"When you are," she says in a soft voice.

Since she no longer cares to keep things quiet, and everyone already knows about us anyway, I drive us over in my truck. It's a short, silent drive. If I had to guess, we've both got a case of nerves, but for different reasons. I'm stressed out over tonight, and she's likely worried about her decision for us to be seen together. I give her thigh a squeeze before swinging my door open. She meets me at the front of the truck before I can get around to open her door like I figured she would. But I jolt in surprise when she takes my hand and squeezes it a few times, flashing me a quick smile before letting go.

"It's going to be great," she reassures me. "I'm going to go get everything done in the stables and then I'll come find you to see if you need anything."

"Joy, you don't have to work extra hard to prove anything to anyone."

Grabbing my arm, she pulls me to a stop just before we reach the stables. "I'm not coming to find you as a hardworking ranch hand. I'm going to come find you as your girl."

She says the words without hesitation, but her cheeks begin to flush, and she swallows hard. I randomly told her I loved her for the first time today, but she's worried about calling herself my girl. God, I really do love her.

"I'll see you later," I say before kissing her on the cheek and heading for my office in the main house.

It still feels strange just walking right in and heading for the office. Every person I pass just nods like I've always been here and always been in charge. Gary is already in there waiting, sitting in the chair opposite the desk, his long gray hair hanging over as he leans back with his hands clasped to support his head.

"You all set?" he asks without turning around.

Smiling, I nod as if he can see me. "Yeah. Ready as I'm going to be."

When I enter the office and round the desk, he grins at me. It's hard to say if he's happy for me, or just excited that this night puts him closer to moving to where he and Rhonda's hearts are. He's been talking about retiring out in the Southwest for as long as I can remember, and as stressful as this change has been, I'm genuinely happy for them.

"It'll be fine. This place might not run itself, but everyone's been here long enough to know what to do when it comes to the rodeo and the bull riding events. This will end up the easy part, you'll see."

All I can do is hope he's right while we go over a few things before I make my rounds. I'm grateful for his help and support until I can find some permanent help. Grayson hasn't said no. He hasn't said yes, but there's hope at least. I'm not delusional enough to think working together will be easy, but at least I can trust him to do right by the ranch and the livestock. *If* he says yes. The more Gary goes over things, the more I relax realizing I already know all of this. I could recite the order of events in my sleep.

It's about time to get the night started and my palms begin to sweat as I head toward the arena. Right on time, the announcer begins to speak and the screens light up as he welcomes everyone to the Cole County Rodeo. It'll be the first time since I can remember that neither myself nor my brother are announced as competitors.

I walk out last, after each competitor is announced and am surprised to be greeted with cheers and applause. I take off my hat and wave while everyone files out of the arena so the events can begin. And as loud as the crowd is, that's what begins to calm my nerves. That, and when I look up, I see Joy standing at her usual spot, smiling at me like I'm the only person here.

Chapter 33

Tate

Trees rush by in a blur of green as I drive back to my ranch after what feels like the longest day ever. And it isn't even over. I'm fucking exhausted. The rodeo went off without a hitch. Well. Almost. After the events wrapped up, we had a bull get injured. The event was over, so most of the staff, including the vet, had gone. Meaning chaos ensued. Those animals are my responsibility, so it was late by the time I finally made it home which means I'm behind. On everything.

As soon as I finished morning chores, I went back over to Boulder Ranch to take a look at every gate to make sure nothing else was missed. The injury shouldn't have happened, and it can't happen again. It won't happen again. I should have been home by now, but while I was still at Boulder Ranch, I heard from Grayson. Finally.

Making my way down the long private drive leading to my ranch, I'm surprised to see Joy's car parked near the barn. And surprised again to find her sitting on my porch with a book in hand. Like she belongs here. Hell, she does belong here as far as I'm concerned.

"What are you doing here?" I ask while climbing the handful of steps leading to my porch.

My front porch isn't as nice as Grayson's, but it's bigger. It runs the entire length of the house and has two rocking chairs, and a small outdoor table set. But Joy really completes it.

"It's good to see you too," she teases as she stands to greet me.

She's casual in a pair of leggings and a loose-fitting top. I drag my gaze over her before leaning in for a quick kiss. The short contact is enough to boost my mood.

"I'm happy to see you. Just surprised. Reading anything good?"

She smiles and holds up a weathered-looking book. The cover is worn, and the pages are slightly bent. "Just my favorite comfort read. I saw you weren't here, and I had it in my bag so..."

"Can you stay?"

She glances down at a large tote. "I can. If you want me to. You look exhausted, is everything okay?"

Recalling the conversation I just finished with Grayson, I nod my head. "Yeah. Actually, I think it might be."

I laugh at the confused look on her face, pick up her tote bag, and gesture toward the door. She has no idea how loaded of a question she asked. Following me into my bedroom, she sets her book on the end of the bed, which I stare longingly at. Without a word, she steps closer to me and places both hands on my chest.

"You look about ready to fall over. Why don't we climb into bed, and you can tell me all about it before you get some sleep."

I step back to look at her. "It's three in the afternoon. I can't go to bed. There's dinner, and evening chores and—"

Pressing her lips to mine, she interrupts me in the best possible way. I don't even remember my arguments as she deepens the kiss, her fingers working quickly to undo the buttons on my shirt. Her hands scorch my flesh as she drags them up my naked chest and over my shoulders as she eases my shirt off.

"Let me worry about dinner. And I'll feed the horses if that'll help."

I open my mouth to argue, but her glare shuts me right up. Instead of arguing, I undo my belt, flip the button on my jeans and slide my zipper down, holding her gaze the entire time.

"Don't look at me like that. I said sleep."

I let out a low chuckle as I slide my jeans off and give her a pointed look. She pulls her top over her head before slipping out of her leggings. She is perfection, standing before me in a simple white bra and panty set. The contrast accentuates her rich brown skin, and I immediately regret agreeing to sleep. I may be dead tired, but I'm not dead.

We both crawl into bed and I pull her into my arms, holding her close as I tell her about my day and about Gray. He asked me to meet him in town to talk. I figured he was going to finally tell me hell no he wouldn't help, but I was wrong. I'm relieved. But I'm also worried now that it's becoming a reality. I guess between missing last night and the bull getting hurt, he came to a decision.

"He's going to help me out behind the scenes. It's more the day-to-day part that I need help with, so it won't get in the way of bull riding," I explain.

"Wow."

"Yeah," I agree. "I didn't think he'd say yes, but I guess things change. The conversation went so much better than I expected. He even mentioned plans to propose to River."

Joy's mouth drops open briefly before she snaps it closed and grins. "Oh yeah? Damn, that's great! I'm not really surprised, considering how inseparable they are. I'm happy for them."

"So am I," I muse. "Oh. And it looks like that bull is going to be fine."

She sags against me, relieved. I felt bad sending her home, but I knew we would be a while. There was no need for her to wait around at all hours of the night. Mostly, I felt bad because I wanted to take her out to celebrate after. Or take her home to celebrate...

"I think that means last night was a success," she says softly.

"Yeah. I mean it could have been worse."

Shifting to look at me, she holds my gaze. "Tate, you've been around long enough to know shit like that happens. It just sucks because it was your first night."

She's right. I lean down to kiss her cheek before pulling her back to me. Her skin is soft and warm. Comforting. Thinking about her words, I allow myself to relax as I focus on the feel of her body against mine. Of course, she's right. Shit happens. But things worked out. I'll have help. There's another month before I'll have the rodeo to deal with, and by then I'll have things settled on all the other fronts. I know how to run a ranch. I've done it most of my life. And now that I won't be running two ranches and a rodeo, things will certainly be looking up. It's that thought that finally allows me to close my eyes and relax, drifting off to the sound of Joy's soft breathing.

Chapter 34

Joy

"I might be getting used to taking a nap and then waking up to dinner," Tate says with a grin.

It's been about a week since I showed up with a tote bag filled with a few items, and I haven't been home since. Grayson has been learning what to do at Boulder Ranch, but since he's only been cleared to do so much, Tate's hours are still long.

"Don't get too used to it. Once your schedule goes back to normal, I'll be expecting long rides on horseback and dinners by the fire out back."

Tate tilts his head back and laughs. His eyes crease at the corners and his dimples are on full display. I could kick myself for all the time I wasted trying to fight my feelings.

"You okay?" he asks when I stare at him a bit too long.

"Yeah. Just glad I decided to stop worrying about other people."

He takes in a slow breath and nods in agreement while reaching for a plate. I watch in silence as he fills it before passing it to me. Pork chops, mashed potatoes, and green beans. It's been a while since I've cooked a large meal, and I figured no better day to do it than Sunday. After passing me a plate, he serves himself.

"Thank you for cooking."

Standing on my tiptoes, I give him a quick kiss just as my phone begins vibrating in my pocket. Ignoring it, I place it face-down on the table and we make quiet conversation while we eat. It's delicious if I must say so myself, and I revel in his praise and smile of appreciation. My phone rings again, but I ignore it until Tate gives me a pointed look and nods in the direction of the device vibrating on the table.

"I'm sure it can wait," I say with a shrug. "We're eating. I'll call them back."

"They've called more than once; it could be important."

"I didn't look; it might not even be the same person."

Leaning back in his chair, he folds his arms across his chest and lets out a low chuckle. The sound goes straight to my core, but I shake it off and flip my phone over, frowning in concern when I see my aunt's name as it immediately starts to ring again.

Mouthing an apology, I stand and step away from the table to take the call. "Hello?"

"Joy, honey. How are you?" my aunt's rich voice greets me.

"I'm fine. Is everything okay Aunt Sophia?"

My chest tightens when she hesitates, and I look up to meet Tate's concerned gaze. He's sitting at the table still, but all his focus is on me. After what feels like an eternity, my aunt finally responds to my question.

"Yeah, I'm fine. I just haven't heard from you and wanted to hear your voice."

I don't believe her for two seconds. I can count on one hand the number of times she's called me just to say hello. Actually, I don't even need my entire hand to count.

"You never call me out of the blue. Did something happen? My parents okay?"

I hear her loud sigh on the other end of the phone. "Everyone is fine. I was just wondering how you are, and if you really like it way out there. I miss you."

Now I'm even more at a loss. This is so unlike her. She's a good person, but she's not the sweet motherly type. She's worked with animals all her life and doesn't put up with anyone's shit. Including family.

"Yeah, Aunt Sophia, I really do like it here."

Tate stands from the table but doesn't move any closer. I give him a quick nod, and he makes his way to me, placing a comforting hand on the small of my back.

"Well. Your mom said you're down there burning the candle at both ends, cleaning horse stalls at some raggedy ranch because the doctor's office doesn't even pay you enough to live on. I don't see why you had to run off in the first place."

I stiffen, even though I doubt Tate could hear her. But still. She called me up just to question my decision to move here, and after all this time? I try not to let her piss me off. I know how she can be. I loved spending time with her as a kid—and I still do—but her way has always been the only right way. And her opinion, the only one valid.

"I didn't run off anywhere. I simply moved here. It's not like I up and disappeared. And like I said, I really like it."

She huffs. "You deserve better than that. I always thought you would end up taking this place over for me."

What? I find myself holding my phone out and staring at it in disbelief. Tate's comforting caress snaps me out of it, and I place the phone back to my ear.

"Okay, tell me what's really going on. You've never said anything about wanting to pass the torch to me. And you've never been this interested in my job."

Another heavy sigh. "It's just that you spent enough time around here and working with me that you can do better. If you want to work with animals, you should be here with me where at least you'll get treated right. And then you can take the place over."

"What are you talking about?" I ask as calmly as possible. "Both places I work treat me extremely well. And I'm happy here. In fact, I met someone, and he makes me happier than I've ever been."

Tate stares at me, eyes wide with surprise, and it hits me that I just announced our relationship. To my family. If my aunt knows, the entire family will know within moments of us getting off the phone. And I don't even care.

"I was in town at the grocery store, and I ran into—" she pauses for so long I don't think she's going to finish what she's saying. "I ran into you-know-who at the store and he asked me if you were okay. Said you just left out of nowhere and he hadn't seen or spoken to you. I asked your mom, and she told me you're over there working two jobs and damn near killing yourself just to survive."

"I'm fine, I promise. Mom's just not happy that I moved away. And he's full of shit because I ended things with him weeks before I even considered moving. I moved here because Rayna loves it, and told me they needed help where she works. I'm not working two full-time jobs. They are both part time."

Tate shoots me a look and my lips tug into a smirk. The ranch is beyond full-time at this point, but my aunt doesn't need to know that. She's all fired up as it is.

"Would it make you feel any better if I came to visit? So you can see with your own eyes that I'm fine. I'm not working myself to death." I purposely avoid Tate's gaze. We're both working ourselves to death. But it's only temporary. "You'll see that I'm happy."

"If you want to move back, you can stay with me. There's plenty of room and I really do need the help around here," she says, completely ignoring what I said.

"Aunt Sophia..."

"Fine," she grits out. "If you say you're happy, I can't argue with you. But come visit so I can see your face. And bring that man with you. When are you coming?"

"When... am I coming?" I look Tate's way, panicking slightly because I know we're both too busy to get away. He's struggling to take care of both places as it is.

"Next week," he says softly, giving me a shrug.

My eyes widen, and I tilt my head toward him in question. Silence stretches over the phone as she waits for my response. Tate nods at me, silently emphasizing his words.

"Um. Next weekend?" My answer comes out as a question.

"Perfect! Oh, I can't wait to see you. And I can show you how easy it would be to just live and work here. Okay, honey, I'll let you go."

As soon as I end the call, I spin to face Tate. "Next week? How?"

"It's not that far. We can get away for a few hours."

"No. She's going to want us to stay for the weekend. I know her. If it's more than a twenty-minute drive, she acts like you survived the Oregon Trail just to get there."

Tate lets out a snort before pulling me into his arms and kissing the top of my head. Instantly, my nerves relax, and I nearly forget I just agreed to bring Tate home to meet my family. My relationship with my parents is complicated, so Aunt Sophia's opinion is really the only one that I'm worried about.

"That's fine. We can go there Saturday afternoon and come back Sunday morning if she asks us to stay." He kisses my forehead. "Just fix one of your amazing breakfasts and she'll forgive us for not staying the entire day. Between Hayden and Grayson, along with the ranch hands who come and go, I'm sure they can keep things over here covered. I'm sure Hayden will be fine coming here unless he has travel plans I don't know about. And I'm hoping Gray will be okay to take care of Boulder Ranch for a day or two."

He's like my personal bubble. When his arms are around me, the idea of bringing him to meet my family isn't terrifying. He gives me a tight squeeze before stepping back and holding me at arm's length while he studies me. Apparently satisfied with what he sees, he pulls me back into his arms without another word.

"Do you even want to meet my family?"

"If you're okay with it, I'd love to meet your aunt and whoever else ends up there."

I laugh because he has no idea how accurate that statement is. My aunt doesn't care that I don't really get along with most of my family. She'll invite them all anyway. Tate doesn't think it's a big deal, but he doesn't know how dysfunctional my family is. I'm not sure if I'm more nervous or excited. I'm only excited because I know my aunt is going to love him, and I have some tiny bit of hope that the rest of my family will be too busy to show up.

"I guess that makes this real, huh? Meeting my family?"

"Darlin', this has been real since the first time you stepped onto my ranch."

Chapter 35

Tate

"Are you sure you want to do this?" Joy asks as I pull my truck onto the road, following the directions on my phone.

Instead of responding, I roll my eyes and laugh. She's asked that question at least seventy times since her aunt invited us. I would have thought after spending nearly the entire week together she would be feeling better about it. Especially since things finally seem to be falling into place. Gray is pretty self-sufficient, so I was able to get ahead on my end before we left. And my hours haven't been as long.

"You're right," she says with a sigh, causing me to chuckle again. "It's fine."

She's sitting up in her seat clasping and unclasping her hands. Anxiety radiates from her as she stares straight ahead. I'm surprisingly calm, considering I never thought I'd be here. In a relationship. Meeting family. I never imagined this was something I'd want or something I deserve. But as I drive toward Joy's hometown, the warmth in my chest is proof that this has been my missing piece.

Keeping one hand on the wheel, I cover her hands with my larger one. She begins to relax under my touch as I make slow circles with my thumb. Once she finally relaxes in her seat, I move my hand to her thigh and give it a squeeze.

"It's going to be fine. And if you decide you want to leave, we'll leave. I'll follow your lead. Do we need a safe word?"

She snorts out a laugh and whips around to face me. "Tate!"

I shrug innocently. "What?"

Her laughter fills the truck, and I feel the air surrounding us get a bit lighter. I understand why she's nervous. It makes perfect sense. We haven't been seeing each other for long. I'm technically her boss. And Joy's aunt only found out about me a week ago.

The two-hour drive did not feel like two hours. When I glance at the map and it says we're only ten minutes away, I can't believe it. It was a comfortable drive once Joy began to relax. We talked and listened to music. Joy sang along to her favorite songs. We are just leaving the suburbs and entering a more rural section of town when Joy tells me to slow down.

"Turn right just past these trees. If you follow the directions navigation tells you, you'll miss the driveway."

As promised, as soon as I pass the trees, a long driveway comes into view. I turn off into the section in front of a large white farmhouse. It's larger than mine, but about the same age if I had to guess. A large fenced-in area can be seen at the end of the curved driveway. Beside the fenced area sits a large barn and stables. It's impressive. I wouldn't have guessed the size of the facility just looking at the driveway and the part of the house that's visible from the road.

"You ready?" I ask.

She shrugs her shoulders and moves to exit the truck, but I raise my hand signaling for her to stop as I reach for my own door handle. She knows I hate it when she opens her own door. And I'm definitely not going to have her do it when I know her aunt is watching, just hoping for a reason to dislike me. I open her door and take her hand, giving it a comforting squeeze before helping her step out.

"Hey, Aunt Sophia," Joy greets as we approach the porch steps.

The older woman was on the porch waiting before Joy had both feet on the ground. Her brown skin is smooth aside from a few faint smile lines and creases around her eyes when she smiles warmly at her niece. Her salt and pepper hair is styled in long braids and piled on top of her head. She's casual in a long flowy top paired with jeans and cowboy boots. She somehow reminds me of Martha, even though she's quite a bit older.

Sophia pulls Joy into a hug, and I wait at the bottom of the steps to give them some space to say hello. Swallowing hard,

I'm unable to tear my gaze from the way they look at each other lovingly. I'm reminded that I don't really have this. The closest I have to extended family is the Eglestons, and I'm grateful to have them... but it's not the same.

"You must be the one Joy was talking about," Sophia says with her hands on her hips.

I remove my hat and reach out a hand. "Tate. It's nice to meet you, Mrs.—"

"Call me Sophia," she interrupts while giving me a firm shake with her weathered hands.

"It's nice to meet you, Sophia," I say with a genuine smile. "Thanks for having me."

"Well come on in. No need to stand out on this porch all night."

Joy takes my hand, and we follow her aunt. The inside is about what I would imagine. An open floor design reveals a large living room and dining room with older, comfortable-looking furniture. The furniture isn't new but it's in great condition. We walk past the farmhouse-style kitchen and into a hallway.

"The bathroom is here." Sofia points to the first door on the right. Across the hall, an open door leads to a dark room. "And that's my office."

We continue down the hall on an unexpected tour. I guess I shouldn't be surprised, but I was under the impression that

Sophia wasn't thrilled to hear about me. While she wasn't exactly celebrating, she seems nice enough. Joy's soft hand squeezes mine, and I find her looking up at me with a worried expression when we stop outside of the next door.

"And this is the guest bedroom." Sophia glances at our empty hands. "You don't plan to stay? It's such a long drive; I thought you'd be here for the weekend."

A smile tugs at my lips when Joy laughingly interrupts. "We have a bag in the truck. I knew you wouldn't want us making the long trip back."

"Okay. Well." She turns and leads the way to the living room without another word.

This time when I glance at Joy, she too is trying not to laugh. We take a seat on the couch and Sophia joins us a couple minutes later carrying a tray with a pitcher of iced tea along with cheese and crackers. She sits in the upholstered chair across from us and watches us quietly.

"So, this is Tate," Joy says awkwardly.

"We've met," Sophia says with the faintest hint of a smirk.

"Well. You see that he's real. And I'm alive. Feel better now?"

"He doesn't seem like your type," Sophia points out. "Where did you two meet?"

Joy coughs and I drape my arm across her shoulders, pulling her close. Of course, her aunt would ask the thing Joy was most worried about first. I can tell Sophia is the type who hates bullshit and can spot it from a mile away. So, I opt for a version of the truth. I don't want to tell her we officially met at a bar.

"We met at the rodeo, ma'am. Actually, that's not true," I say, correcting myself. "Technically, we met in the parking lot where she works."

Sophia looks between the two of us and sits forward expectantly. Shrugging, I look to Joy to tell the story, figuring I won't do it justice.

"I was on my way to meet Rayna for lunch, and *someone* wasn't paying attention to what he was doing and backed into my car."

The old woman gasps in horror, so I raise my hands in defense. "She's fine. Her car is fine. I wasn't going that fast. But she's right. My mind was somewhere else. And I'm glad it was."

"You're glad you backed into my niece's car?" she says, incredulous.

"Yeah. If I didn't, we might not have met. And that would be a damn shame."

Grinning, Sophia holds my gaze for several long moments before flicking her eyes to Joy. "I like him. Now, what's this about the rodeo?"

Chapter 36

Joy

Perfect. I knew I could count on Aunt Sophia to ask me the one thing I wished she would avoid as soon as she got the chance. I was hoping to have her as in love with Tate as I am before slipping in that small detail. If we lied, she'd probably never know. But I'm not going to do that. I really want her to like him, and that's not the way to do it. She'd know something wasn't right.

"Well, Tate is a bronc rider. He was leaving the doctor's office after having his hand looked at and that's when he backed into me. I didn't know who he was, and I let him have it for hitting my car. It was opening night of the Cole County rodeo, and the arena was the first time I saw him again after knowing who he was. Eventually, we talked, and I discovered he was actually nice. Not just some big jerk who backed into me."

Tate's shoulder bumps mine as he laughs. "You thought I was a big jerk?"

His eyes bore into me, and the sexy smirk on his face nearly makes me forget myself. "The biggest."

My gaze drifts from his eyes to his lips and back. I want to kiss those lips, but the sound of my aunt clearing her throat reminds me where we are. Heat rises to my cheeks at my wayward thoughts, but I'm less anxious than I had been a few minutes ago. I'm not sure if it's Tate's presence that calms me, or my aunt's reaction.

"So, a bronc rider from the ranch you work at?" Sophia clarifies.

"Well... he isn't a bronc rider anymore."

She looks at me, confused. "You said he's a bronc rider and that's how you met."

"Yeah. Well. I guess he technically is, but he owns the ranch." I wring my hands while I wait for her to understand what I'm saying.

When she crosses her arms and sits back in her chair, eyes narrowed as she watches us carefully, I know she's figuring it all out. Not wanting to be the first to speak, I sit back and try my best to keep from fidgeting as I wait for her to say something. Anything.

"Well, that's one way to get in your boss's good graces..."

"Aunt Sophia!"

Heat rises to my cheeks, and I can't tell if it's anger, embarrassment, or a combination of both. Before I can respond, my aunt's face splits into a grin, and she smacks the arm of her chair.

"Relax, I'm kidding. I feel better knowing he's a ranch owner and not one fall away from the poor house."

Oh my god. I didn't think this could possibly go worse than I imagined, but here we are. I don't even have a response to what she just said. Leave it to her to find a way to compliment the man and insult him all at the same time. Humiliation threatens to consume me as my entire body heats.

"That's understandable," Tate says after a beat. "I've been running my family ranch since my father passed away fifteen years ago. And when I took it over, I also had my younger brother to look after since he was only seventeen. Climbing the ranks in the PBR was fun, but those days are long gone. I couldn't afford to be just an injury away from disaster. Not when it was all up to me to keep the ranch going. I only have Boulder Ranch because the owner came to me personally and asked if I would be interested in taking it over."

Tate's response is much more cool, calm, and collected than what I wanted to say to her. My anger hasn't completely dissolved, even as my aunt looks at Tate like Jesus is back. It's obvious she was just testing him, but she didn't need to be so insulting. Tate's warm grasp on my thigh is the only thing keeping me from snapping at her, even though the conversation has already moved on.

"I am so sorry," I whisper when my aunt finally retreats to the kitchen to finish cooking.

"She just wants what's best for you. I'd be worried if she wasn't concerned about some cowboy sweeping her niece off her feet," he says as he stands and pulls me up. "I'm going to grab our bags from the truck."

That makes me laugh. I hadn't thought about it like that. City girl moves to the country and gets mixed up with some no-good cowboy. I get it. If it was my daughter, I'd be beyond suspicious. And there have been times when Aunt Sophia was more of a mother than my actual mom, so I suppose it makes sense, but it doesn't stop me from feeling completely mortified. When she'd said those things to Tate, I wanted nothing more than to disappear.

With the hope of calming my nerves, I make my way to the small bathroom. I'm hoping a hot shower will settle my nerves, plus it'll be nice to freshen up after sitting in the car.

"Mind if I join you?"

Tate is standing in the doorway, leaning against the frame as he drinks me in. My heart pounds from the way his heated gaze scorches every inch of my naked body. Obviously, he's seen me naked before, but there's something about being in my aunt's house that makes me want to cover up. It feels like he shouldn't be standing here.

"My aunt is just in the other room," I whisper.

"So?"

"So, we can't be doing that when she is right there."

Smirking, Tate stalks toward me until he's only inches away. "So? She's not in here. Anyway, I was just talking about a shower. I'm sure your aunt wouldn't have a problem with us freshening up before dinner. Would she?"

I shake my head, unable to form words when all my focus is on his fingers as they work at the buttons of his shirt. The muscles of his chest and torso move and flex as he maneuvers the fabric over his shoulders.

"No," I breathe. "It's polite to freshen up for dinner. You're right."

He hums as his hands move down to his belt. That simple act has heat pooling between my legs. I may have said we can't do anything with my aunt a couple of rooms away, but all I can think about is the way his hands feel on my body. He pulls his pants and underwear off in one step and my gaze stops at his semi-erect dick.

"Get in," he says in a low voice.

Licking my lips, I turn around and step into the shower. Hot water sprays over me as I move to the front to give Tate space. The shower isn't big enough for two people to comfortably fit, but that only means no one is left standing in the cold. The thought of the way we must look squeezing into the small space makes me giggle, and I cover my mouth to keep quiet.

"Something funny?" Tate asks.

I look up into his teasing gaze and shake my head, before turning it into a nod. "We don't both fit in here. I'm sure we look ridiculous."

He smiles. Really smiles. His dimples show as deep creases and his eyes crinkle around the edges. I can't look away. I can barely breathe. His laugh is a soft rumble against my shoulder where it's pressed against his chest.

"I think we look perfect."

My eyes snap to his when he grips my waist and pulls me to him, his hardening cock a promise against my stomach. I part my lips to speak, but he captures them in a kiss, causing me to forget any arguments I may have had.

"Turn around."

Already trembling from anticipation, I do as he said and turn to face the shower spray. I hear a click and then a few seconds later his hands are on me, squeezing and stroking as he lathers me up. Each innocent swipe of his fingers fuels my arousal. I need him to touch me. I need him to do more than just touch me.

When he finally reaches my center, his fingers gently cleanse me before moving on to my thighs and the rest of my legs. I feel no shame when I whimper in disappointment. Not even when he laughs at me.

"My turn."

When I turn around, he hands me the body wash. I snatch it, ignoring the smug smile on his face, and begin washing him. Running my hands over his body, gently exploring every last inch is proving to be as arousing as when he washed me. My hands reach his stomach, and his sharp breath is nearly my undoing.

Continuing down his body, my hands reach his hard cock. I lift my gaze to his and find him watching me closely with his jaw clenched like he's fighting the same battle I am. With a slow breath, I continue down his body until he's completely clean. His cock is at eye level, and after briefly meeting his gaze, I lick my lips and focus my attention in front of me. I want to taste him. I lean forward, but before I can get my mouth on him, he grips my arms and hauls me to my feet.

"Please," I whimper.

He shakes his head. "Not yet. We have to go spend time with your aunt and give her a chance to get comfortable with us. And not get pissed if she has some questions. When we're done, I'll let you touch me. I'll let you come."

I open my mouth to argue, but he once again interrupts me with a kiss. His kiss is hungry, and I match his need as I swipe my tongue along his. I'm left needing more when he finally pulls away and steps out of the shower.

As I get dressed, I realize the feeling of need has completely canceled out any worries about dinner and what else my aunt might say. I don't care what she does, I just want it to be over so he can follow through on his promise.

Chapter 37

Joy

Aunt Sophia continues to pile food onto my plate after I said it was plenty. "You're getting too thin; you need to eat."

Looking down at myself, I don't even try to mask my laughter. No one in their right mind would ever consider me too thin... but I'm not exactly watching my figure, either. My eye roll is subtle as I wait for her to finish piling on more and more food I'll never eat. Tate watches me with a small smile and it's enough for me to forget my irritation.

"Everything looks delicious," Tate says quietly. "Thank you."

My aunt smiles, melting under his praise, and I use the opportunity to set down my plate before she can continue to add more. When we joined her in the kitchen, my aunt seemed to be much more relaxed and in a better mood than she had been in the living room. She cooked her famous fried chicken and macaroni and cheese along with green beans from her garden.

She does her own canning, so even from a jar, they are a million times better than anything you can find at the store.

"Oh, my goodness," I say around a bite of food. "This is so good."

It is good. Better than anything I've had in ages. Food distracts me, and it isn't long before we've all finished without pausing for conversation. My aunt stands and clears our plates before I can even process what's happening. She returns with a pot of coffee, and I help myself.

"So, have you retired from riding?" my aunt asks.

Tate finishes pouring his coffee and takes a sip before responding. "I'll probably step in as a pickup man when I can, but other than the one event I travel for, I think I'm done competing."

It's my turn to squeeze his thigh. So much of his life was spent competing at Boulder Ranch, it's got to be hard to give that up. Even when giving it up means ensuring other young men get the same opportunities he had when he was first starting out.

"Why do you travel for that one event?" she asks. I feel like I'm sitting in on an interview, but I don't know how to make it stop. Tate doesn't seem too uncomfortable, so I let him speak for himself.

"They're like family. When I can't ride anymore, I'll still go there every year. Hell, I'd be the rodeo clown if they asked me."

This earns him a laugh. Not just the respectful chuckle that she usually gives. Aunt Sophia covers her mouth so she can laugh without being ridiculously loud. It must be contagious because I find myself laughing even though it's not all that funny.

"Have you dated other women who work at the ranch?"

"Aunt Sophia!" I scold, but Tate is shaking his head, holding a hand over mine.

"No ma'am. It's been some time since I've dated anyone seriously." He answers easily.

Sofia clasps her stiff, wrinkled hands in front of herself. I wait for her to say something else, but she just sits back, eventually sipping her coffee. Following her lead, I sip my own. Tate does the same, and I assume the conversation is over until my aunt speaks again.

"Too busy taking care of everyone else?"

He freezes before physically shaking off her question. "Pretty much."

"Well..." She pauses for a long moment. "You deserve to be happy. Stop taking care of everyone else and take care of yourself for a change. That's the only way you'll ever make someone happy."

We're both left staring after her when she gets up and heads to the kitchen entrance. "I cooked. You two can have cleanup duty."

And then she's gone. Looking over at Tate, I shrug and begin picking up the remaining dishes from the table. She washed the pots and pans as she went, so there's not much cleanup left. Turning the water as hot as I can stand it, I fill up one side of the sink so we can wash the handful of dishes.

"Thanks for coming with me."

Tate looks at me, confusion etched across his features. "Why wouldn't I come with you? I'm the whole reason she demanded to see you. And she said something I needed to hear, so thank *you.*"

I wash the largest serving dish and then pass it to Tate to rinse and dry. I want to ask him to elaborate, but I feel like he would have if he wanted me to know. So, I keep quiet as we fall into a practiced rhythm of washing the dishes. We've cleaned up his kitchen together enough times for it to feel like second nature. I leave him to wash the last few dishes in the sink while I put the food away and bring over the last few dishes from the table.

"This is nice," he says softly.

I turn to find him wiping down the sink before draping the cloth over the faucet. "Cleaning?"

He laughs and I allow my smirk to spread to a grin. "Family time. It's nice. It's been a while..."

Instantly, my heart aches for him. I'm not close to my family, but I couldn't imagine not having them. A couple of times a year, we get together for an uncomfortable meal. My parents come to show their displeasure, and my aunt makes sure to ask every possible question she can come up with. It's basically a family tradition. If he sticks around, he'll see for himself that family time is sometimes better in theory.

My chest constricts with disappointment. I was dreading my parents showing up during the time I was specifically planning to spend with my aunt, but I feel like Tate would have liked to meet them, as awful as the interaction would have been. It's peaceful without them here, but I can't help but worry that Tate will take it personally.

"What is it, sweetheart?" His low voice breaks through the silence.

"Huh? Nothing. Everything is fine, why?"

"You aren't a good liar. Just tell me what's bothering you." His silky voice wraps around me, causing me to immediately forget the trepidation I'd been feeling.

"My parents didn't show up," I say with an exasperated sigh. "I'm sorry they didn't, but don't take it personally. It's better this way."

His eyes lock on mine. "I'm not arguing with you, but you don't look relieved. You look disappointed."

"I guess I'm not making a lot of sense, huh? We aren't close and barely get along... but they should have wanted to meet you. I'm sure they know we're here." I shrug, not really knowing how else to explain it.

"Well, I'm not offended or anything. It's been a good day."

"It has," I agree.

He places a quick kiss on the top of my head before threading his fingers with mine and leaning close to my ear. "Let's get to bed. I have a promise to keep."

Chapter 38

Tate

It's crazy what a difference a couple of weeks can make. Things had been moving forward with Joy before our trip to see her aunt, but it still managed to change everything. I needed someone to tell me it's okay to be happy. It's okay to take care of myself. Hearing Sophia's words eased the guilt I'd been fighting since I stopped denying my feelings.

Now, here I am locking up my office and it's only 2:30 in the afternoon. Things seem to be falling into place, and I'm not sure if I should be relieved or worried. All I know is it feels amazing to work normal hours again. The rodeo is only a few days away, but everything is good to go. Again, I should probably be worried.

"Heading out, boss?"

I stop at the gate beside Hayden. "That hasn't gotten old yet?"

"No, boss, it hasn't," he replies with a shit-eating grin.

"Yes, I'm heading out. Did you need something? Other than a reminder that you don't actually work for me here. And you've worked with me on my ranch for years..."

Hayden laughs even as his gaze remains fixed on the roping team getting in some practice. "Nah. A bunch of us are going out Friday night if you're interested. Should be fun since you could run this place in your sleep now."

I snort. "I wouldn't say all that. But anyway, I have a date Friday night. Maybe next time."

Hayden's lip twitches and I walk away before he can give me shit. He knows I never was big on going out before and after the events. I would usually show my face a few times, but that's it. I'd probably decline even if I didn't have someone better to spend my time with.

"Heading out?"

This time I'm surprised to see Gray approaching. He's got his keys in hand, so I assume he's on his way out, as well. I don't give a shit what hours he works, as long as everything gets done. Surprisingly, we've been working well together. Our tasks don't overlap, so that helps.

"Yeah. You know how it is, get out when you can. I have a couple afternoon meetings tomorrow." I'm not sure why I feel the need to explain myself. "You heading out?"

"Yeah. Plans with River. Anyway, we're still down a pickup man for this weekend. I can do it Friday if I have to, but that doesn't solve Saturday," he explains as we head to the gravel parking lot.

"I can do Saturday."

Gray looks at me, surprised. I'm not sure why, we've teamed up as pickup men a lot over the years. Obviously, I'm not riding, so it's not any more of a big deal than Gray doing it Friday night.

"Why are you looking at me like that?" I ask in annoyance.

"I just thought you were stepping away."

"I am from bronc riding. I'm not going to compete in an event I'm hosting. But it'll be nice to get in there and participate."

Gray shrugs before walking to his truck. We may work well together, but it's still awkward as fuck. I'm just glad we can be around each other, and no one needs any x-rays. Even after stopping to talk on my way out, I manage to get dinner into the oven and everything else I need to do finished before Joy gets off work. She's still spending nearly every night here even though our schedules have freed up a lot.

Glancing at my watch, I find I still have about an hour before Joy is expected, and for the first time ever, there's nothing I should be doing. I prop my feet up on the coffee table, lean back on the couch, and flip through channels until I find something to waste time on.

"Something smells good."

I hadn't even heard her come in. She places a kiss on my forehead before sitting beside me and reaching for the remote. Laughing to myself, I wait for her to find something she likes.

"Move in with me," I blurt out, because apparently when it's something important, I have no filter.

Joy freezes for a moment before slowly turning to look at me. I know what I said was pretty sudden, but her look of surprise is comical. Her eyes are wide, and she opens her mouth several times before closing it without a word.

"You spend most of your nights here, anyway. I hate that you come with a bag like a visitor. I want your stuff here. I want you to have a few drawers that eventually turn into you taking over my entire dresser. I want your shit all over the sink. Well..." I pause, giving her a pointed look. "I think you already have that last part down."

Leaning to the side, she nudges me with her shoulder. "You're joking like this isn't a big deal."

"Because it isn't," I say simply. "The last time you slept at your house, I stayed with you. And it was terrible because I had to wake up ridiculously early, and I didn't like leaving your house before dawn. We already know we don't like sleeping apart. It's the next logical step."

Her lips pull into a grin as she continues to look at me like I've escaped the insane asylum. I've never felt saner, or more sure about anything. I want her with me all the time. The thought of sleeping alone causes a dull ache in my chest.

"The next logical step?" she echoes.

"Mm-hmm," I mutter, pulling her close. "There's a roast in the oven, by the way. That's what smells good. I was hoping we could eat out back. By the fire."

She watches me in silence for what feels like an eternity. Her eyes study me, lingering on my mouth before returning to meet my gaze. Using my thumb, I make a slow back-and-forth motion against her forearm where I have a gentle grip on her. When I rushed home to get dinner in the oven, it wasn't so I could ask her to move in. I just wanted to surprise her with dinner out back like our first date. But when she came in and snatched the remote like she belongs here, I had to make it so. I want her to belong here. To take over my space. To take over my life.

"Okay," she finally says. "But under one condition."

I shift in my seat to get a better look at her. "Okay, and what's that?"

"I quit."

Chapter 39

Joy

I never knew something could feel both strange and undoubtedly right. Tate pulls his truck into his normal parking spot and looks at me for a moment before killing the ignition and stepping out. My eyes follow him as he rounds the truck to my door as usual. He looks so good wearing a simple button-down shirt and dark-wash jeans along with his usual cowboy boots and hat. But while it feels strange coming for the rodeo without having to work, being here to support Tate however he needs me feels right.

"You ready?" he asks, reaching out a hand to help me step down.

"Sure am, Mr. Garrison."

He pulls me close, a hint of a chuckle rumbling through his chest, and gives me a quick kiss. The rodeo has nothing to do with me anymore, but I still put on my good jeans and boots. Since I'm not here to work, I'll just pretend my job is to look good on Tate's arm. I laugh at the thought.

"You good?" he teases.

"Yeah. Just thinking about my job."

He stops and gently tugs my arm, so I turn to face him. "Your job here? You quit, remember? Didn't even give two weeks' notice."

"Your arm candy. A trophy girlfriend." There's no use trying to suppress my laugh as I do a slow twirl. "I've never had this position before, so I'm hoping I can pull it off."

Tate's laugh is deep and rich as he signals for me to spin once more. When I'm finished, he pulls me close and kisses me. His laugh tickles my lips, and I cup his face in both my hands, holding him still so I can kiss him once more before we leave the parking lot, and our little private moment comes to an end.

"You are definitely pulling it off. I was paying more attention to you than the road for the entire drive here."

"Good thing it was a short drive," I tease.

"Very good thing," he agrees.

He takes my hand, and we walk past the barn and stable and into the main house to his office. Gary and Rhonda are both already waiting in the small seating area outside the offices. Rhonda is gorgeous as always in a long, flowy top with the shoulders cut out and boot-cut jeans, looking like a true rodeo queen. As soon as she sees us, her face splits into a grin.

"Hi! Joy, you look beautiful," Rhonda gushes as she stands and pulls me into a warm hug. "I couldn't believe it when Gary told me you quit."

"Oh, you know how it is, I'm sure. I totally plan on stepping up to work anyway while I'm here. If I see something needs done, I can't just ignore it."

"And there's always something to do, that's for sure! Come, let's go have a glass of wine before any of that work tries to catch us."

Tate and Gary both laugh and shake their heads as they head into the office. I've never just hung out with Rhonda before, and I hate that this will likely be the first and last time, unless they come visit during rodeo season. She leads me down the hall and to a set of French doors. Opening them, she gestures for me to step into the elegantly decorated room.

It looks like the farmhouse aesthetic that is in all the magazines. The walls are a light sandy color, while the fixtures and the furniture are dark, providing a nice contrast. Decorative pillows and blankets in various pastels give the room an inviting feel. She opens a small wine fridge and fills two glasses about halfway.

"I hate that we've never done this before." Rhonda raises a glass. "To new lives."

We both take a sip. "Are you excited to move?"

She nods enthusiastically, taking another sip of her wine. "Yes! We love it over there. And I'm so ready to be done with the cold winters. What about you? What do you think of all this? A lot of changes for you. Especially if things are serious between you and Tate."

My face heats at the mention of Tate and me. There's no more denying how serious we are. Especially once I officially move out of my place. It's a small town. Everyone will know when I move. The cat will be all the way out of the bag when my new address is a certain ranch that borders Boulder Ranch.

"Tate asked me to move in." I squeeze my eyes closed and wait for her reaction, but there's nothing but silence. I open my eyes, and she's smiling at me, patiently waiting for me to continue. "That's why I quit. I know it's stupid, but I can't live with him and be on the payroll. I can't fill your shoes, though, so I'm not sure what I was thinking."

Laughing, Rhonda waves me off. "Don't be silly. Don't worry about my shoes, just fill your own. By the time we're unpacked in our new house, Cole County will have forgotten all about us. Especially with you and Tate running things. Yes. *You* and Tate."

For the first time today, I feel myself begin to relax. If Rhonda thinks I can do this, maybe I'm not crazy. Maybe I am exactly where I need to be. We chatter on about nothing and everything while we finish our wine. By the time we leave her office, Tate walks out of his office with Gary behind him.

"You ready, sweetheart? It's about time." Tate reaches for my hand as soon as I'm close. "Walk out with me for the opening ceremony?"

My smile grows as I consider his request. "Okay. Yeah. Let's do this."

Chapter 40

Tate

We did it. We fucking did it. Things are so much better than last month, it's hard to believe this is only the second rodeo since I officially took over. I lead my horse to the gate where Joy is standing with Rayna and wait for Grayson to come bursting from the chute. It's his first night back on a bull since his accident, and I'm not sure who's more nervous, me or him.

"He's going to do great," Joy says from across the gate.

I give her a curious look, because I haven't said how nervous I am to watch him ride. I don't think I've been this nervous even before my own rides. There's no point asking how she knows what's going through my head. All I can do is hope I'm putting on a good enough show for everyone else to believe I'm fine. Riding as a pickup man helped take my mind off it for most of the night, but now I want to crawl out of my skin.

Gray's eyes meet mine from across the arena and I'm completely locked in when he nods his head to signal that he's ready. Fortunately, my horse knows what to do and stays in position to get to work if need be because I'm frozen in place as I watch. I don't breathe. For eight seconds, I remain mostly still while Gray holds on tight to the rope with one hand and holds the other one up as the bull bucks and spins, sending dirt and slobber flying everywhere. For eight seconds I cease to exist.

The buzzer sounds, and Gray frees his hand, jumping to safety with the biggest smile on his face. As soon as I'm beside the bull, he takes off through the gate and into the pen. Tears sting my eyes as I watch Grayson celebrate. It was a hell of a ride. I'm proud of him. It takes a lot of heart to go out that strong the first time following a serious injury.

One of the ranch hands gets my horse into her stall and taken care of, so I make it back to the arena in time to catch the line-up. Gripping Joy's hand, I lead her out to the arena where we congratulate each contestant. Joy's smile is as wide as mine when they announce Gray's score. He shakes my hand and then surprises us both by pulling Joy in for a hug. Fucker. But I step back, cutting my eyes at him as soon as he looks at me.

"Did you see that? He killed it out there!" Joy shouts in excitement.

"He did. And so did we."

She looks at me with one eyebrow raised. "We?"

"Yup. Everything went without a hitch. I wasn't running around. Everyone loved you. I'm sure Gray will be celebrating with his fiancé. What do you say we do the same?"

"Tate, it's too dark for a ride."

I glance over at her and my gaze lingers at the way her eyes shine in the dim lights from the barn. It is dark, but I know the land like the back of my hand. So do the animals. We'll be fine.

"You scared?" I tease. "The moon's full, so it won't be completely dark. Anyway, these horses know the way. They'll get us there without any problem. They don't even need our help."

Joy studies me before looking ahead into the darkness. "Fine. But don't let my aunt fool you. If I go missing, you'll go missing."

Leaning to one side, I huff out a laugh while taking the reins with one hand. I have no doubt she's telling the truth. In fact, I was worried I was about to go missing for the first part of our trip to see Ms. Sophia. She may look like a sweet old lady from afar, but I'm certain she can and would kick some ass.

"Stop pretending like you don't trust me," I say with a laugh. "Come on; let's go before we lose moonlight."

That makes her snort with laughter. We aren't going far, and I make sure to keep my horse at a slow pace since Joy isn't comfortable. The path is visible in front of us, but seeing things without a trace of daylight makes everything look completely different. I don't stop sneaking glances at Joy, and I can tell from her small smile that she left her worries at the barn.

It only takes us ten minutes to get to the spot. This small piece of land, although it isn't far from the house, is the perfect place to view the pastures in the daytime. Here in the darkness, everything is cast in shadow, but you can still make out the silhouettes of the livestock.

I have a blanket already set out and candles ready to be lit along with a lantern, so we aren't completely in the dark. The picnic basket is filled with her favorite snacks, and I grabbed a bottle of wine and two glasses from inside the house. I wanted to make tonight special. I already asked her to move in, but I don't need a reason to do something nice for her. I've finally realized that just doing the right thing isn't any way to let someone know how I feel. It's a lesson I should have learned years ago, but I was too stubborn to pay attention.

"What's all this?" She carefully dismounts and makes her way to the blanket.

"Just a little something to celebrate." I flip on the lantern and then light the candles.

"What are we celebrating?"

"Everything?" I light the last candle and shrug. "Us. Moving in together. A successful rodeo. You quitting your job…"

She laughs. "You know I didn't really quit. I just quit getting paid."

She isn't lying. The past few mornings, she woke up with me and went into the ranch to help out. And when I reminded her that she didn't work there anymore, she told me she didn't have to listen to me because it wasn't like I could fire her.

"Well, whatever you want to call it. I said the most important part first. Us. Nothing else matters."

"Tate…"

"I'm serious. I know everything has been crazy pretty much from the moment we met, but I wouldn't change it. This is all new to me, and I realize I haven't been good at telling people how I feel. I think they should just know because I did something nice. Something ordinary." Making space between my thighs, I pull her to sit between them.

"Tate, I know how you feel," she says gently.

"And I'm going to make sure you never doubt it. I'll always do things for you to show how I feel. I've been this way for too many years for that to change. But I'll be sure to do things like this, too. Because I want to."

She stiffens in my arms, and when I place a finger beneath her chin to tilt her face toward me, I'm horrified to see tears. At a loss for words, I wipe them away and stare at her in a panic. I'm not sure if I've said too much, or maybe the wrong thing altogether.

"What's wrong?" I ask when she still hasn't said anything. "Did I say the wrong thing?"

She shakes her head emphatically, her curls swaying behind her. "No. You said just the right thing. I've always assumed you never really know when you're with the right one. If they treat you okay and you get along, it's probably fine. But now I know." She takes in a ragged breath. "Now I know."

I place a kiss on her damp cheek before pulling her to me. Her back is to my chest, and she covers my arms with hers as I hold her tight. Unlike her, I never thought I wanted this. I never imagined I could have something like this. But even without having anything to compare this to, I know she's the one. I know this is it.

"I love you," I say against her ear.

"I love you, too. So much."

Acknowledgements

Holy Crap. This will be my seventh book in just over a year. If it wasn't for my readers, I wouldn't be here. Thank you all for supporting a small indie author.

Thank you Street Team for supporting me and hyping me up while also hyping up my book and getting excited about my next release. Also to my ARC readers: you are amazing. Thank you everyone who leaves a review. Reviews are super important so thank you for taking the time to leave one.

I also wouldn't be here if it wasn't for the support of my friends and family, and especially my writing family. Roberts Row let's go! (even if this one is your fault) For anyone who follows me on social media, you probably know all about Roberts Row. If you don't follow me, you should. It's sometimes entertaining, but always… something. Just ask Vanessa, the president, founder, and sole member of our unofficial fan club.

Last but not least, if it wasn't for my family being so understanding when I'm locked in my writing cave or away at a signing, I wouldn't be able to do this. Thank you for putting up with me.

About the Author

Ashley Willow lives in a small town in Ohio where the only excitement is whatever she creates while burning the midnight oil. If she isn't writing romance, she's reading it. Her childhood hobby was "writing better versions" of her favorite books (now known to be fanfic), including the fabulous smut that got her grounded as a pre-teen. Oops.

When she isn't writing or busy with her nose in a book, she is spending time with her family. Her happy place is anywhere with salt water, and bonus points if she can combine that happy place with books, writing, and her family. She is currently working on a new manuscript, so there is more to come!

Feel free to send her an email with any questions or comments: authorashleywillow@gmail.com

Follow her on social media: @ashleywillowwrites on all platforms.

Also by Ashley Willow

Stars of Life Series

Stars of Life

Tests of Fate

Calls of Need

New Beginnings Duology

Bryce

Logan

Standalone

Her Way Home

COMING SOON:

Love Me (Boulder Ranch Series)

Hunt Me (Boulder Ranch Series)

Want Me by Britton Brinkley (Boulder Ranch)

Save Me by Britton Brinkley (Boulder Ranch)

The Darkest Light- A Dark Mafia Romance

Made in the USA
Columbia, SC
03 July 2025

60065700R00169